Nothing To Be Afraid Of

S. A. Wooderson

MARTIN IN THE WOODS

PUBLISHING

Contents

Chapter 1

The Fly Garden

The relationship between humans and the plant world has always been strong. They feed us and our animals through fruits, grains and grasses, trees shelter and cool us, and flowers feed the bees and make life possible. It is a natural cooperation. But the agreement that a wronged woman and an agave plant come to will be a special sort of partnership that will benefit them both.

I moved after we sold the house. After the realtor sold the house I'd spent so many years getting perfect. It was the house where the kids had grown up, where my youth had died, and after the divorce he wanted his half to travel and chase tail. All the equity just sitting there, he said, as if it had all just miraculously happened. As if I hadn't worked sixty hours a week and put every spare penny into paying off the mortgage. I'd always thought that owning your own home, owning it outright without a mortgage around your neck, was freedom.

Turns out freedom is forcing the former love of your life to sell her home so that you can go to a nudist retreat in the desert and tan your junk with your newest girlfriend. So, I moved. Moved out of the suburbs and into an ungentrified urban refuge where only I spoke English and nothing else. The house was small and old, but the lot was large, and I could afford it. I knew the real estate value would go up because the yuppies were gentrifying everything, even the streets formerly only known as places to pick up crack whores. I wonder if he ever visited a whore when we were married. He seemed to date a lot of them now that we were divorced. Well, not divorced. It wasn't final yet, that damn waiting period like we were going to change our minds and suddenly get back together. I was still so angry the only reason I could think to see him at all would be to "accidentally" knife him, or force-feed him Almond Roca candies till his allergy kicked in and he died choking on sugar, chocolate and his own bile.

These were the things I thought about as I worked in the garden. I'd bought the house for the garden with its large old fruit trees planted long ago by some long-dead peasant. This was a peasant's house in a neighborhood of immigrants and peasants where everyone helps everyone else and there is the certain knowledge that money and food will always be scarce so you do what you can to survive. You plant food, not petunias, and you keep a chicken or two. I was considering getting chickens. All my neighbors had them, and it seemed only fair. The trees in front shaded the front doorstep and the old rosebush near the door grew sweet red roses with the dark fragrance of lust.

The backyard had a large raised bed garden running alongside the back of the house. Up on the raised bed grew aloes and agave. Everything else on the property served a purpose: fruit for eating, peppers for seasoning, roses for beauty. I wondered what purpose the huge old blue agave had. Perhaps the original owners had made their own tequila; I was sure they hadn't made agave syrup like the hipsters these days used to sweeten their lattes. The agave and I had an unhappy peace. I kept cutting, diminishing it, cutting off the spiny needles of death. I cut the pointy tips off the agave's leaves to keep myself from being skewered by the spines and, while doing it, got scratched and caught by the ones I had not yet cut.

I hung a hammock in the backyard to enjoy my warm sun, trying to tan my cellulite-scarred veiny legs. I found myself remembering my old legs. The legs I'd thought were too big, too heavy, too curvy. The legs he'd never said anything nice about. The legs of a woman twenty pounds lighter and twenty years younger than me. The legs I had never appreciated that I missed so much now. Still, these old heavy stumps carried me about well enough. With compression socks, I could stay on my feet for at least three hours before I needed to sit and rest. Three hours was enough to mow the lawns or paint a room. The grass in the back garden had died from neglect while in escrow, so that was my job now that I had finished my jobs inside the house. Not that I'd managed to do much. There wasn't much budget, but at least I'd painted my room so it was no longer the off-white of a rental apartment.

The only thing I couldn't control were the flies. They would bother me while I lay in the hammock at the back, buzzing around. I wasn't sure where they came from. They just seemed to have arrived with the summer and hadn't left. I couldn't find any maggots or any reason why they were there. I took a look over my neighbors' fence to see if they had something on the other side that was causing them, but their yards were much cleaner and better organized than mine. I could only aspire to have the neat vegetable garden and prolific fruit trees of my neighbors. So, I kept working on the garden, and it kept me from letting my anger consume me.

Rachel, my oldest daughter, came by. She brought me a present. A rototiller, and a café latte. I enjoy my coffee so much more now that it isn't something he expects me to share with him. Just a sip, he'd say, or even grab it without asking. I started getting the largest size and swallowing as much as I could before I sat it down, because the moment I sat it down, he'd grab the cup and finish it. He never allowed me to have anything that was mine.

And now I do. I have this garden and a rototiller. So now I can break up all the dirt and replant the grass on that patch of yard that's slightly harder than concrete. She'd made sure to get me one that plugged in rather than one with an engine. Strange, sometimes I think she doesn't listen to me at all, then she buys me exactly what I want. I hate gas-powered garden devices. All those years I spent in the garden fighting with the lawnmower, just trying to pull the cord and make it start. Apparently, all my screaming was memorable. Usually, I would put off mowing the lawn too long, put it off because I didn't think it was my job.

I didn't think it should be my job. He'd promise to do it. And I'd wait. I'd beg for a lawn service, and he'd say he could do it. Of course, he didn't. Finally, when the grass got too high and the neighbors started to look at me funny, I would pull that old mower out. And pull on the cord and curse. And pull on the cord and scream. And pull on the cord and rant until finally my rage would enable me to pull the cord fast enough and hard enough to start the old machine in a cloud of blue gas smoke and obscenities. For all the things she remembers about her youth differently than I do, this is one area she and I have the same memories. I hate two-stroke engines. She couldn't stay long, of course. If she'd stayed too long, we would have fought. We always fight. She's always had to be on his side. When she was four and he smacked her for throwing her food on the ground, she bit me. When he cheated, somehow it was the person who had stayed faithful who was at fault. She was always angry at me, not him. Somehow, even when I wasn't in the room, it was my fault. And now that he's running off to get screwed by strange women her age it's also my fault. My failure as a woman. I didn't keep her daddy from being the tail chaser he's become.

The rage has been helping me get the place in shape pretty fast. At least there's that. The rototiller and I broke up the backyard in three days. And I planted the grass seed, scattering it like the guy on YouTube said you should. I wasn't going to buy a machine just to throw grass seed out. Then there was the water. Two, three times a day, sprinkling it lightly and hoping.

The longer I work in the garden, the more I see muscles I've never seen before. I haven't spent a lot of time lying in that hammock, although I think the fly trap I bought is bringing the flies down a little. I spend my days moving and, more and more, I see a physical strength I have never possessed. I think it was that newfound strength that gave me the idea I could remove that agave.

That and the spike that skewered my right hand, which took a week to heal.

I figured the easiest way to get it out would be to cut it back as much as possible and then dig outside it. Giving it some room, cut a foot or so outside where I figured the roots had spread to. I bought a battery-powered saw and started cutting off the huge leaves. The spikes up and down the sides required gloves, and I worked on it for three days, every day going to bed with more scratches and wounds. But honestly, what else did I have to do?

Day four I had nothing but a root system and a couple of new center leaves left and I tried digging into it but I couldn't get more than a half inch down. So I went out another couple of feet. I figured I would dig out the side of it, then lever it out. I hit something hard two feet down. I figured it was a big stone. I'd been pulling out little stones as I went, and even pieces of concrete. It was like whoever had filled this raised bed had just thrown in whatever they had to fill it up. They definitely hadn't bought bags of Amend organic raised bed soil from Home Depot at $8 a bag. I mean, I understood; it seemed insane to be buying dirt, especially since it cost so much and was such a bitch to carry home. It's one thing when the store will load it into your car for you, but you're still the one who has to lug that damn bag back out of the trunk and move it around the garden to where you need it. I guessed the bags must weigh damn near 50 pounds each, and that's before they got wet. Anyway, obviously whoever had made this raised bed didn't have those kinds of resources. I was half expecting to find garbage and old tin cans in there somewhere. Whatever I had hit was hard, really hard, maybe like a piece of metal. I reached my hand into the hole. It was definitely hard. Smooth. Maybe a piece of concrete, maybe a paint can or something like that. I just started to dig in earnest. I stood on the raised bed and shoveled the dirt out of the bed and onto the lawn.

At some point, I realized how big this thing was. It was down between three and four feet and I reached down to scrape away some dirt to see what it was and whether I could lift it. I wondered if I'd need to hire a man to help me pull this damn aloe out. I pushed the dirt away slowly, and it wasn't a piece of concrete. It was pale colored, and it was connected. It was a rib. Damn, someone must have buried their pet in the raised bed. Made sense; easier than digging a hole. I pushed a little more dirt away. It must have been a huge dog, maybe like a rottweiler, because it was not just almost as wide as the raised garden but almost as long. I reached up under the roots of the aloe and scraped away more dirt with my fingers.

I was covered in dirt now, my hands bleeding from the minor scrapes and my fingernails black with dirt. I pulled away some more dirt and realized what type of animal it was. In front of me was the hand of a man. The skeletal hand, larger than my own, with most of the joints still lying where they had fallen.

It took me a minute to remove myself from standing on the corpse. Standing on the ground, I stared at the hand. Definitely human. Definitely a man.

This wasn't a raised garden. This was a burial plot. Flies buzzed around my head. There was nothing left for them to feast on. The body had been buried too long ago. I looked up and understood the purpose of the agave. The agave kept the dead from being disturbed. I thought about calling the police.

I could just see it. I'd be on the news. The police would arrive with sirens and guns and noise. My new neighbors would come out to see the kerfuffle. This wasn't a neighborhood where you called the police, so they would think the police were there to arrest me. The cops would walk in en masse with their big boots and walk all over my new grass seed.

I looked around at the fragile grass seed hatchlings. The rototiller had let them root, and I'd spent every day for two weeks watering the seeds, protecting them from birds. And it would all be turned into mud, then dust. Then I'd have to start again. Rototill and buy grass seed again, and it was almost summer. It would be impossible to grow it once the temperatures reached the 90s.

I looked down at the skeleton. His head was still buried under the agave. The roots of the plant probably went down through the skull. I started to giggle, imagining a skull with spikes, a different kind of Day of the Dead ornament. The police would pull out the agave, that was sure. I wouldn't have to hire someone to take it out. But how much damage would they do in return? If I ever wanted to sell the property, would I have to declare there'd been a corpse in the back garden?

My phone rang. It was the ex. "Yes," I said in a voice without emotion. I had found a skeleton and my coping mechanism was to be calm, too calm. Calm enough to speak to my ex. "Hey, do you have the Waterford Crystal?"

The stuff my godmother gave us as a wedding present? I thought, then answered monosyllabically. "Yes."

"I need it back. If that's ok? I mean, you don't drink and I do, and I have grown accustomed to drinking out of those glasses. I thought that I had them but when I unpacked at the new place, well, I went through all the boxes and I couldn't find them. And well, I meant to call you a while ago..."

And I got accustomed to sleeping with someone. I got accustomed to sleeping with you. Do you know how long it took me to sleep in an empty bed? Do you know I still can't sleep on your side? And how do you know I don't drink? I don't, but how dare you presume I am the same weak person you left a year ago?

"Lynda really thought it would be nice to have the crystal..." So Lynda was the newest one. She must have been the one who unpacked. He would never have unpacked everything. She must be old enough to know to ask for nice things.

"Lynda's out of town for a week or two, visiting her mom. I could come over and pick it up today."

"Yes," I said.

"Ok, thanks. I'll be over in a few hours."

"Ok," I said and hung up. A few hours.

I looked down at the hole. I would need to dig out some more.

There was enough time to go to Home Depot and get a coffee.

I needed a couple more fly traps, a few bags of soil, a couple more agave plants, and an extra-large almond milk latte before he arrived.

Chapter 2

Gridley

There are towns all over the southwest United States like Gridley. Off the beaten path, baking in the heat of a frightened century, watching people leave and leave their possessions behind. Their possessions, and often their pain. But as these towns empty and drift toward decay and death, there are strange things that can fill the empty places. And those things may speak to the living.

Thirty miles south of Paradise. This really shouldn't be the best way to describe a town. But it was that type of town. The town of Gridley, thirty miles south of Paradise, CA. It was the type of town that no one plans to go to. You ended up there because your car broke down on the way to the Mammoth Mountain ski fields or because you turned off the highway to find food and got irrevocably lost. It was not a town you looked for, rather one that finds you. Susannah Walston had been there for nine months. She'd gone on purpose, running away, as always. This time she even knew what she was running away from—his name was John. Gridley seemed like the perfect place to disappear.

She'd gotten a job easily enough. After all, no one came to Gridley. They only left. So there were plenty of wanted signs—one at the café out on the highway and one at the antique store in town. The antique store was one of the few stores left on the strip, the rest of them boarded-up reminders of what smalltown America used to be. No one shopped in Gridley anymore. Everyone drove out to the Walmart Supercenter in Yuba City. Even the people who talked about the good old days and how Walmart had killed the town could be found having a Big Mac for the road before they left the Walmart parking lot with a week's worth of groceries and that new pair of jeans. The antique store was right across the street from the church, which was the only other place with any business on the street.

She took both jobs. The job at the café, and at the antique store where she saw many of the same people each day, older people who'd left the farm to the kids and moved to the town, women abandoned by age and death living out the last of their days praying to God to ease their pain, and paying a tip to the waitress to fill their coffee cup just so they can have her stand by the table one more minute—paying just to be able to interact, at least for a moment, with another human being.

And then, when they were gone, their things made their way to the antique store. She'd been hired because she understood the internet enough to sell things on eBay without being one of those young punk kids who, obviously, would find it unacceptable to man the desk at the Brooks and Sons Antique Emporium.

Mr. Brooks, her boss, was the last of the sons, and when he was gone, the store would be too. He'd explained it to her quietly the first day when he hired her. "Normally, you understand, I work the counter. I have for some time now but... well, I'm getting on..." She wondered how many of the antiques were actually as old as he was "... and my doctor... he's been suggesting I should slow down some. I've heard from my daughter there's something on the computer network thing I should use to sell some of my better items, and that's why I'm looking for someone. Jennifer—that's my daughter—she assures me that I need to do this. She can't help me, of course. She's quite successful, you know, she's an attorney in Los Angeles and she just had her first children, twins you know, at forty-two... the wonders of modern science. She sent me a photo... it's around here somewhere..."

"I can work the computer, Mr. Brooks. I know how to sell things on the internet."

"Ah yes, internet. She said something about an auction?"

"eBay."

"Quite. I'll need you from ten till two Tuesday through Saturday. We're not open on Monday, and of course, we've never opened on Sunday."

"Of course."

"Well then, it's all settled. That is, if you're available?"

She assured him she was. She could work Sunday and Monday and nights at the café. It would keep her busy. Busy was good, less time to think, so she started at the store the next day.

By the third week, he was leaving her alone much of the time at the store. There were few customers—only the occasional lost tourist looking for something cheap to ship back to his pretentious neo-classic McMansion—and Mr. Brooks finally trusted her enough that he started to come in late and leave at lunchtime so he could stroll home to make himself lunch and potter in the garden.

She'd needed his help in the beginning to judge the value of all the items, the antique desks, the Queen Anne tables. She found it all dark and creepy, dusty, and yet fascinating. With orange oil polish she found under the bathroom sink that looked like it had been bought in the late 80s, she started to polish the furniture one piece at a time. At first, so the pictures on eBay would look better, and later because it was something to do. And something was better than nothing. Susanna didn't want time to think. She needed to keep her hands busy; she needed to keep moving to drown out the sound of scurrying fears in her own head.

If she hadn't been polishing, she wouldn't have found the secret drawer in the underside of the old desk. It opened with a creak, and she pulled out the dusty yellow envelopes. She wondered for a moment if she should wait for Mr. Brooks before she opened them. She put them on the desk and stared at them for a moment. Mr. Brooks would be in the next morning. There was no point waiting for him; they were just letters, after all. She'd show them to him when he came in. Odds were they weren't valuable, just some old personal letters.

She turned the envelope over. It had her name on it. To Susannah Walston. That was her name, her real name. Not the one she used now. Not the one that Mr. Brooks used. Not the one she had told everyone. This was her real name, not Suzie Chalmers, the one she used to try to hide, not the one on the ID she was using.

Her breathing sped up. She was scared. This was her real name. No one knew her real name. It was the one thing she had left. Her name had power over her, if anyone knew, if John knew. If someone knew her name, it would be too dangerous. But there was no way these letters were for her. They were old, so old. The paper was dry, yellow and cracking, the ink faded. It was just a strange coincidence. But now she was curious. It was a sign she should just take a peek.

She opened the first one slowly, careful not to break the paper as she opened it. The paper was so old and difficult to remove from the envelope. Yellowed by time, but somehow she knew she was the first person to ever read it.

Dear Susannah,

I am glad I could finally reach you. This letter is for you, Susannah Walston—or Suzie Chalmers if you prefer that name now. This is not a coincidence. When you leave the antique store tonight, do not go home. John has found you. He is coming to kill you. Go to the police, tell them you heard a noise in the house and did not enter. They will find him pawing through your underwear with a gun.

Tomorrow, when this has all come to pass, read the next letter.

The letter was not signed.

Susannah looked around. She was alone. No one was playing a prank on her. No one knew her true name. No one knew about John. She looked down again at the letter, so old it was crumbling in her hands.

Susannah read it again. Then, being a sensible woman, she started to shake.

Running to her car she dialed 911 as she ran. She unlocked the door, climbed within, hit the central lock device and felt safer. As if glass windows could shield her from the world. Could shield her from her past. The letter was still clutched in her hand and she started to read it again. It took a second before she realized 911 had answered. "911, what is the nature of your emergency?"

"There's someone in my house.""Are you certain?""Yes.""Are you at the house right now?"

"No, but I heard he was there. You have to go. The address is 31 Oakwood Drive, Apartment 4. It's my ex-boyfriend. He's trying to kill me."

"Ma'am, stay calm. I am dispatching a car to the scene. Please do not enter the house."Susannah turned the key on in the car. "I am not going to enter the house," she said and drove slowly back to her apartment.

The police were arriving at the same time. The front door was open; he'd broken one of the panes of glass and opened it. She sat in the car watching as the police entered the house and dragged John out.

She read the letter again, then crumbled it in her hands and put the next letter in her glovebox for tomorrow.

Chapter 3

Allergic

We live our lives with unwritten contracts. We agree to oxygen, gravity, Newtonian and Einsteinian laws, whether we know them or not.

We deal with relationships, money, motion. But what happens when reality breaks a contract? When, little by little, the rules dissolve and life refuses to cooperate. James isn't prepared for what is about to happen to him.

But then, would any of us be?

I thought it was a bug. You know, a little time praying to the porcelain gods, a little time spent sitting on the throne, and I'd be fine. And maybe even thinner. At 40 it's not as easy to keep the "not a beer belly yet" in check. And since Janice had left, I'd realized I needed to drop 10 pounds if I was ever going to get a babe on Tinder, or however they do it these days.

The third round of this had taken me to urgent care. I'd been pushed into a room to wait. The walls were that color of green that was supposed to make you calm but instead made you think of all the times you'd squished broccoli sprouts into your pants just so you wouldn't have to eat them. Then flushed them after dinner. I only broke the plumbing once doing that.

"Mr. Harris," said the doctor, a cute little Latina probably young enough to think I was a dirty old man. How did you become a doctor so young? "We will take some tests and see what we can do for you. Meanwhile, fill the prescription. It should stop the vomiting. And make sure to drink lots of fluids."

Yep, pretty slick here. I am at urgent care, looking at the posters about UTIs and wondering if the doctor is single, and she was looking at me like I was an infectious disease. What a thought. Who knows? It seemed kind of possible.

I was back a week later for the results. All I'd kept down all week had been dry toast and water. And the symptoms weren't getting any better. I'd pretty much soiled myself on the drive over, and it was only two blocks.

"Well, Mr. Harris," said the young doctor, "it looks like it's a food allergy."

"Well, what am I allergic to? I'm not eating much now..."

"We are going to put you on a Low FODMAPs diet and see if we can find what is triggering your symptoms. Have you ever had any other allergies?"

"Hay fever. I take an antihistamine and I'm fine."

"That probably isn't related."

She gave me a list of foods I couldn't eat, which was a lot longer than the one I could, and told me to keep a food diary and come back in a couple of weeks. FODMAPs, it turns out, wasn't some trendy way of saying something dirty. It was a list of food containing sugars that were hard to digest (fermentable oligosaccharides, disaccharides, monosaccharides and polyols to be exact, because that just rolls off the tongue). Sometimes it's hard not to be a nerd, so I fell down the rabbit hole for the next two hours just reading everything—no onions, no fruit, no dairy, no bread, no fucking nothing. When the list of what you can eat is shorter than the list of what you can't, life is pretty sad.

No more meeting the guys at the pub for a drink and a cheeseburger. No more drinks after work at all, no more donuts in the office. You know you are pretty sick when you look at the list of all the things you have been told to give up and you give in.

By Saturday I was feeling well enough to join Eric for a round of golf, then back to the 19th hole, and I sipped soda water and ate some unfried potatoes. In case you've never tried them, potatoes not cooked in oil are a tasteless mushy abomination. And after lunch I didn't puke. Which was a nice change.

There is nothing more painful than vomiting. It's a violation that knows few equals. You lose control and are forced into submission, retching and heaving until it ends, and you pray for death. Not that this ever kept me from drinking to excess when I was a kid, but as a kid you have to learn the hard way, and alcohol has a knack of making you forget just enough to do it again. I remember one day waking up with a particularly bad hangover on the floor of the toilet. I don't remember exactly how I got there, but by the vomit in the john and my hair and on my clothes, it was obviously unpleasant.

This was not like the horrid self-induced illnesses of my youth. This was somehow more terrifying, more absorbing, for there was no cause, no reason for it, and no idea that it would end. When I'd been hung over as a young man, waking in my own sick on the floor, I knew it would be over soon. All I had to do was survive. But how can one survive when there is no end in sight and no idea what caused it in the first place?

And for the next three weeks, I was great. And then I got to start introducing things again. Eggs came up in colors of yellow and green. So that was a no. Avoiding them was harder than I thought. No more muffins, no more breakfasts.

That was two years ago now. And I had gotten used to it, until a year ago, and then the pain and vomiting began again. So, back to the doctor for more tests. The next diagnosis was Celiac disease. Elimination diet, then reintroduction, then biopsy, and no more gluten, no more bread. No more pasta. You don't realize how much pasta you eat until you can't eat it anymore. And gluten-free pasta is almost, but not quite, like eating gooey sawdust. And gluten-free bread is a poor excuse for something to hold unpreserved ham and dairy-free cheese together for consumption. But that was ok, because six months ago I started to vomit again.

The smell and taste of sick were old friends. I could feel it coming. I surrendered to it. And I texted my allergist. This time my skin started to itch and swell, and my throat was ticklish. "James," began the allergist. Any time the doctor has actually bothered to look up from their computer screen and look at you, it's not good. The fact that he remembered my name was more of an indication of how often I'd been to see him.

"Yes. What's going on?"

"Well, James, I think I told you when we started down this road that you could become allergic to more and more things."

I nodded, but I couldn't remember that conversation at all. Had he ever really told me that? Why wouldn't I remember if he had?

"Well, you see, your immune system is overactive, and it's reacting to more and more things. We are going to put you on a very bland diet and I'm going to also suggest some medication, and give you an EpiPen in case you have a worse reaction."

"What kind of medication?"

"A steroid regime to start. Let's see if we can lower your immune response. You will take prednisone every day, and a limited diet."

I stared at him. He'd stopped looking at me and was looking down at the paper. "A limited diet... Isn't that what I eat already?"

"For the next couple of weeks I'd like you to eat white rice and chicken."

"White rice?"

"... and chicken. No herbs, no spices..."

"Are you kidding?"

The doctor didn't respond. "I want to see you in two weeks."

"Two weeks." Repeating seemed natural, the act of a stunned animal repeating the sounds it heard.

I thought I'd already given up on everything I could. I thought food wasn't important to me anymore. I thought I had already lost everything that mattered to me. No more eating out with friends. No more drinks after work. I'd lost so much in the last two years. It wasn't just the food; it was everything. I remember hearing my mate say I'd rather die than quit beer. I had died. I was no longer myself. Piece by piece, my life had been pulled away.

It might have been different if I'd been married before all this started. The last girl I dated kissed me and her lipstick had gluten. I'd had to go vomit, which is not the best thing to do on a date. The swelling of my face probably wasn't that attractive either. The girl before had eaten ice cream, before I knew milk was a problem, and the hives I broke out in were far too distracting to get it up, or get it on.

I went home to my place, to my computer where now I lived my life. I worked online now, remotely as they say. A concession for my condition, although my boss was sure I was faking, and slacking off. I could see it in his face in every Zoom meeting. I looked perfectly healthy. What was my excuse? It would have been easier if I could have explained it better.

I wanted to say I've got cancer, or something normal. Not my immune system is reacting to everything, and the smell of your deodorant might make me break out in a rash. I looked around my house. All the things I had gotten rid of, the perfumed cleaners, the leather jackets. White rice and chicken. I looked down at the Epi Pen the doctor had put in my hand when I walked out. He hadn't made me wait in the pharmacy.

"Two weeks and we'll have a video appointment. We will set it up. Take the pills every day and keep this with you."

"Why? I'll only be eating rice and chicken." I put the EpiPen in my pocket.

"If you have any other reaction, call 911 and use the pen."

"Do I call you?"

"Call 911. They can contact me." He pointed to the medical alert bracelet I had on. It was plastic. The metal one I had started with had turned my wrist into a strip of raw and blistered skin when I'd become allergic to metal, somewhere between eggs and milk.

I looked down at the blank and empty floor. No mats, no cat bowl over by the counter. The cat had gone with Janice. I thought we were forever. Sure, I'd never actually married her, but we'd been together for seven years and I thought she understood how I felt. She left at the beginning of all of this, three years ago, when Mr. Perkikins had started making me sneeze. "It was simple," she said, and she walked out with her life packed into three suitcases and a cat cage. "All you had to do was ask me to marry you, to make a commitment."

"Didn't I co-sign this lease with you?"

This wasn't, apparently, the right answer. I'd stopped sneezing after Mr. Perkikins was gone and I'd counted myself lucky. No more cat hair in my bed, no more cat climbing down under the covers in the morning. And I was single and ready to mingle. So I said.

I missed that damn cat. I'd called Janice a few months ago. She was getting married. I didn't get an invitation, even if I could have gone.

She didn't have much to say. "Why did you call, James?"

"Just to say hi."

"I thought about not picking up.""How are you doing?"

"I'm well. I'm getting married next week. I thought maybe you'd heard and that's why you were calling."

"I didn't know. I don't really see any of the old crowd anymore."

"Jamie said that. That you're sick or something."

"Yeah. Don't get out much anymore." And there was nothing more to say. We could have talked for hours once, about nothing, and I would have stopped listening halfway through, nodding just to keep up my side. But now there was nothing, just an empty space. And she didn't need to hear about my problems. So I wished her well on her wedding and hung up, regretting that she'd picked up the phone at all if she really didn't want to speak to me.

I walked to the kitchen and turned on the tap to fill the pot. White rice. And chicken. I opened the fridge and took out the chicken, ignoring the vegetables and margarine that were in there to mock me.

I poured the rice into the pot—instant rice; it would be done soon enough—and put a chicken breast in the toaster oven set to air fry. I opened the fridge from habit to take out a drink, and shut it. No beer, no coke, no wine, no juice. I'd have to drink water.

I grabbed a glass and put it under the water filter. A spot touched my hand and itched, but I didn't think about it. I lifted the glass and drank, and the water hit my throat. Like itchy hairy insects climbing down my windpipe.

I fell to the ground choking, spitting the water out between my swelling lips. I reached out for the EpiPen that had fallen out of my pocket. Out there on the tile floor, just beyond my reach.

Chapter 4

Dearly Departed

This is a story of Love. Of Love and her handmaidens Lust and Longing. They ride the rainbow, and at night move the stars. They can transcend death and time, and when they live inside you then you will never be fully alone, even in the cold darkness of reality. But can you live in that reality?

"Well, I hate to spread bad news but...." If only that were really the truth, I thought, looking at the face of the man I'd wasted ten years of my life with. All he had given me since we met was bad news. News like the woman I dated before you had herpes. Did I forget to tell you? News like it's our 10th anniversary next week and I don't want to be married to you. There was no way this news could be worse, but it was. "I heard that Jimmy was dead."

"Dead?" I couldn't be hearing right. "You mean Jimmy who used to run the shop?"

"Yep. Word is he died of an overdose in Poland. I mean, you know he was in bad shape. I wouldn't put it past him. Dennis told me he didn't like spreading rumors but he'd been told by three different people."

"Oh"

"Yeah, well, that's the rumor anyway."

Rumor, rumor. It had to be false. The last time I saw him couldn't be the last time I ever saw him. He'd been packing to leave for Poland, leave with his wife and kids. After twelve years in Costa Rica, the American surfer boy who had come to the ocean was going to leave with his Polish wife. His marriage was over, but he was hanging on with his wife because he wanted to see his kids. He'd been full of hope, trying to start again, trying to start a new life. I needed to say something. Kevin couldn't know. No one knew. Only Jimmy and I knew what had happened. If anyone else was going to know, it shouldn't be Kevin. The one time Kevin noticed I was upset shouldn't be now. I had to fill the silence before he noticed. Not that he'd ever been terribly perceptive, but even he would notice when the tears started to run down my cheeks. "Well, you know how rumors are around here. I need to go to the bathroom."

I walked off as calmly as I could and didn't let the tears fall until I was well clear of Kevin's view. I allowed myself two minutes to weep. Then I wiped my eyes. Jimmy couldn't be dead. I loved him too much for that. If he had died, surely I would have known it, would have felt the passing with my heart, would have stopped thinking about him every second of the day. I would call the number I had for him as soon as I could. For now, wipe the eyes, put the wall back up around your heart, and walk back out to be pleasant to Kevin. As soon as he had what he wanted, he would leave and then I could call.

"So I want to take the kids next month for the entire weekend. Sofia wants to take them on a trip to Arenal."

"Ok." I nodded. What was he saying? Something about Sofia, that paragon of virtue, the woman who wanted to steal away my children.

"So, it's ok with you if we take them after school on Friday and..."

"Sure, whatever. Just ask the kids if they want to go. I have to get my car fixed anyway in San Jose, so I'll take the opportunity to get a tune-up."

"We'll have them back on Sunday, and they can be at school on Monday."

"That's fine with me. Anything else?"

"No." He walked away, knowing he was dismissed, without saying goodbye. I walked into my office and went to check the time in Poland. It was 1 a.m. I couldn't call now. Too late. I'd have to wait.

I didn't sleep. I couldn't sleep. I went through the motions. I picked the kids up from school, I drove them home, I fed them, I put them to bed. I wasn't really there, just doing what I had to do in order to keep going. To keep going until I knew for sure, until I could call him, until I knew whether he was safe or not.

My heart kept telling me he wasn't dead, couldn't be dead, but my head kept yelling, "Of course he's dead, of course you are just being silly, just like you've been silly this long thinking that one day you two might have a future. The kind of stupidity that keeps you thinking about him every day of your life, the kind of stupidity that makes you dream about a man you've never even kissed, never had a relationship with, rather than start a new relationship with someone real, someone available, someone here.

"You tell yourself that he is the man you love, the only man you love, the only man you have ever loved, but what do you know of him, really? Do you know if he ever felt anything for you?

"When you told him you loved him, what did he say? Did he say he loved you too? No, he said nothing. Just a long cold silence over the phone, which in your embarrassment you wanted to fill with chatter, and you would have, except that he came back with 'Um. I don't know what to say about that.' You'd told him he didn't need to say anything, but you wanted him to, you wanted him to say that he was in love with you as well. He said he was on his way to Poland with his family and you said you understood. You were the understanding one, and then he came back with, 'Well, I suppose that it's nice that someone out there loves me.' And it had to be enough, it had to suffice. And then he left."

I had rehearsed every conversation we could ever have, but now, what if we never spoke again? What if that was it, what if the man I loved was not only gone but dead, buried somewhere? I'd thought of so many things.

Moving to Poland, traveling to Europe just to see him, finding him a job offer he couldn't refuse, something that would bring him back. But when it really came down to it, I'd always believed he'd return. Even if he didn't love me, he loved Costa Rica. He was a creature of the ocean. He fed off the power of the waves and water, and there was no ocean in Poland. How could he ever live there?

And then I started to rehearse the phone call. How did one really start a call like that? "Hey, Jimmy. I heard you were dead, so I thought I'd call to see if you were." Or, yeah, "I know we haven't talked in over a year, but I had to speak to you now because I needed to know you were alive." Or maybe the conversation with his wife, "Yes, hi. This is Anne (does she know I love her husband, that I told him I loved him even while he was living in the same house as her?). Well, hi. I just wondered if Jimmy was available." "Oh, he's dead. Oh, I'm so very sorry." Was there any good way to have this conversation? It didn't matter; I had to know.

Somewhere in the early morning hours I fell asleep, and when I awoke I was late. I made lunch and drove the kids to school in a blinding haze. My body knew the road or we would all have died.

I was too busy dreading my phone call to even notice what the weather was. I got home and went straight to the phone. Jimmy's number. The one I'd kept but never used, knowing that I had no right to call him. Just like I still had his two-dollar bill in my wallet.

I remember the day he got it. He was so excited, like a child. He said it was going to be his good luck charm. He'd folded it carefully and placed it in his wallet. Then, a month or two later, I'd been in a hurry to leave. I had no cash, and I needed some. I asked him if I could borrow some cash. He'd opened his wallet and gave me everything in it. Everything, even his lucky $2 bill. Kevin would never have done that. He would have asked how much I needed, then asked why I needed it, then counted out exactly what I needed after I had sufficiently groveled. Jimmy just gave me everything he had without even asking why I needed it. I'd paid him back that night, paid him back all but the $2 bill. Sure, I'd given him back the value of it, but the bill itself I'd stolen from him. Tucked into a corner of my wallet, now it would be my good luck charm blessed by my love.

I should have given him back the $2 bill. He might have needed the luck more than I did.

My hands shook as I dialed the number. Then I waited while it rang. One ring, two rings, three rings… oh dear God. "Witam." It was a man's voice. It was his voice.

"Hi, Jimmy. It's Anne."

"Oh, Anne, hi. How are you doing?"

"Great." And I was. He was alive and suddenly so was I. Every nerve in my body buzzed with the sound of his voice. I started to shake. I wanted to cry but he wouldn't understand. He was alive. I wanted to scream it out, shout to the whole world: The man I love is ALIVE.

"Did you get my email last week?"

"No. You sent an email last week?" He sent me an email. What did it say? Why did he send it? "I didn't get it."

"Oh, then I've probably messed it up. I hate computers."

"I know. You always did."

"I am doing email now. I have an email address: jimmyz@googlemail.com."

"Oh, great."

"I'm on my way back." He was laughing.

"You are?" I wanted to scream. My hands were shaking so hard I could barely stop them. I sat there just willing myself to keep as calm as I could, to keep talking to him.

"Yes, I'm coming back in two weeks. I've got an appointment with my lawyer and our house needs to be fixed up and rented again."

"Two weeks, wow. How long will you be here?"

"Fifteen days. I hope I can get everything done."

"It'll be good to see you."

"You too. I've got to go."

"Ok, bye. See you soon."

"See you, Anne." And he hung up. Five minutes on the phone and my life was different. The world was beautiful, and I had two weeks to become beautiful. I would exercise, I would diet. I closed up my office and went for a swim, bouncing up and down in the waves, unable to keep from smiling, from laughing. He was coming. He was coming. He had sounded happy to see me.

The next two weeks were a blur. I wrote him an email and when he responded, I rejoiced. When he didn't respond for a day or two, I mourned. I found myself checking my email every half hour just to see if he had sent me anything. A word—that was all I needed. I wanted to be cool and calm, but when he didn't respond for three days I sent him another email. He was busy. He was packing. He was coming. He'd be here soon.

He was flying into San Jose. I rang and got an appointment to get my car fixed. I didn't tell anyone that the real reason I was going to San Jose wasn't to repair the car; it was to see him. I didn't tell anyone else he was coming. This was my secret, my source of joy, and I didn't need anyone, least of all Kevin, interfering. So I smiled, arranged for Kevin to babysit for two nights, and drove my car to San Jose. He didn't have a phone at the house, so I'd told him I would just drive up to the house to meet him.

I dropped the car off to be repaired and took a cab up the mountainside to his house/their house. The last time I'd seen it, the house had been full of life—kids running around, dog in the front yard. Now it looked like an abandoned property, something left for years that was slowly, with disuse, returning to the land. It had an ominous feeling like it was haunted, the kind of strange stagnant energy that ghost towns and empty motels have. He must have heard the vehicle because he came out of the house to greet me.

He looked better than I had seen him look in a long time. He'd dropped some weight and added some muscle in the right places. His hair was short and neat, not like the mop it had been when he had left. He looked beautiful, just as I had imagined in my dreams he would look. I paid the cab driver and jumped out and gave him a hug. He hugged me back, holding me just those couple of seconds extra to tell me what I needed to know, to tell me that he had missed me too. He threw an arm around my shoulder, and we walked into the house together.

The house was as abandoned inside as it had been outside. None of their furniture was there, every sign of their lives in that house was gone, and in its place were only windows that didn't close properly and paintwork that was peeling. Jimmy led me into the kitchen and we sat down on the counters to talk to each other. From across the room, I could feel his eyes on me, warming me, undressing me, and yet we didn't hurry. He talked about everything, about how going to Poland had been a mistake, about how he really needed to return to Costa Rica. I smiled, hoping that one of the reasons he wanted to return was me.

He asked me if I wanted a drink. I said yes. All he had in the house was water, but he brought me a glass and our fingers touched. I looked up at him and he leaned down and kissed me. It was a slow kiss, shallow at first, then demanding more until he was drinking in my soul and I his. He took my hand and led me to his room. It was nothing more than a mattress on the floor, but he'd made the bed, perhaps hoping that I would come and help him unmake it. He pushed me against the door and kissed me again, and then pulled his mouth off mine and down my neck and the top of my breasts, exposed by the camisole I'd worn. I slid my hands up under the back of his shirt and pulled him to me; he pushed me away and pulled my shirt down, breaking the spaghetti strap. He devoured my breast, sucking and biting my eager nipples. I ran my hands over his zipper, but before I could remove his pants, he pushed them away. Lifting me up, he carried me to the mattress and laid me down on it. He withdrew and took off his pants and boxers.

I didn't need foreplay. I'd been waiting two years for this moment. All I wanted was for him to possess me. Tenderness could come later. For now, all I wanted was fulfillment.

I found myself on top. His fingers started to trace lines up and down my thighs. I stripped off my shirt and ran my breasts across the light hair of his chest, riding him slowly back and forth while his fingers made me want to speed up. I kept it slow.

I began to count the freckles on his chest one by one with my tongue. I could sense his response to my tremors. He rolled on top of me, grabbed my hands above my head so I couldn't do anything else with them, then finally we fell asleep wrapped in each other.

He woke me before dawn, one hand on my breast. I pulled him to me, not wanting him to go, and slowly we made love, a slow, gradual climb with kisses, giggling and laughing. We explored each other's bodies until we were both tired and fell asleep for another couple of hours.

I awoke spooned into his arms. He woke and whispered in my ear, "I won't be able to come to the beach to see you."

"I know," I said. The goodbyes were starting already, and I wasn't ready to let go. "My car will be ready at twelve."

"You have to go back." It wasn't a question. We both knew I had to. I'd stolen a day out of my life for him, a day away from my children, away from my business, but I would have to return. I couldn't leave the kids for long. "I don't think..."

I didn't want him to say it; I didn't want to hear it. "You are so beautiful," he said, and I believed it. He was the only person I ever believed that from. I'd married Kevin because I never believed I was beautiful, never believed I was attractive, and when Kevin had never complimented me, it made me think that he was honest. In hindsight, it only meant that he had never really wanted me, never loved me. I wanted to be wanted, desired, loved. I needed to be viewed as something more than a mother, more than a businessperson. Jimmy was the only person who had ever made me feel like a woman, made me feel like I was worthy of love.

I found myself coming, but tears came with the joy. Jimmy would be gone soon and there was nothing I could do about it. I had no right to ask him to stay. If anything, I believed he was doing the right thing.

His kids were in Poland, and how could he abandon them? Jimmy rolled me over and kissed my tears. "Please don't cry," he said. "I want to remember you smiling." And for him, I forced a smile. I wanted to be whatever he wanted. I wanted to be a better person for him, a happier, more adventurous person. He made me feel like I could be the best of myself.

He took my hand and led me to the bathroom, then he placed me in the bath and turned on the warm water. As it caressed my body, he gently massaged my shoulders, then he soaped and massaged my tired, overworked body. I turned around and took the bar of soap, drawing circles on his chest, down his abdomen. I could feel him shudder and fall into me.

"I'm sorry," he said.

"Don't apologize. I'm just happy that you want me. I was so afraid I'd drive out here to see you and you wouldn't want me, that I'd be too fat now to be attractive to you. I know you. I know you prefer your women thinner, more athletic."

"I don't..."

"Yeah, you do. I've watched who catches your eye for years and I'm sorry. I wanted to be perfect for you. I wanted to be everything you could ever want, but there wasn't enough time. I've put on so much weight..."

"Don't start this. I think I demonstrated I want you."

"I'm so happy we had this chance. I've regretted not sleeping with you ever since the day we went for a night swim and you asked me and I said no."

"Why did you say no? Why did you turn me down?"

"'Cause you were so drunk, and my pride wouldn't let me. I didn't want you to just ask me because you were drunk. I wanted you to ask me because you wanted me. And I didn't want to lose you as a friend. I wanted us to be friends forever, no matter what. You know, normally I can tell anyone anything but with you, I always feel like we leave things unsaid... I wanted you to ask me again."

"Um... I wasn't really that drunk, was I?"

"Do you know why everyone believed you were dead? That you'd OD'd? Because we know how miserable your wife makes you. I know you have to go back to her, and I am not asking for anything... really. At least not for me. But you have to move out of her house. Go live on a friend's sofa if that's all you can afford but move out or eventually you will be dead."

"You're starting to turn into a prune."

"Ok, so take me to bed." He lifted me and carried me back to the bed cradled in his arms. The conversation continued. "I love you so much, Jimmy. I don't know why, but I just need you to know. I've never loved anyone the way I love you."

"What do you want me to say?"

"I don't want anything... That's a lie. I don't need anything. I'm not asking you for anything. I've never asked you for anything. It's just that I felt I never had the chance to say goodbye that last time and I needed to say goodbye properly. I just keep wondering where our lives would be if when I was nineteen I'd gone to Costa Rica instead of New York, or when you were nineteen, you'd gone to New Zealand instead of Costa Rica. I know we would be good together; I know we could have a great life together. If you asked me, I'd fly to Poland with you and make a new life for myself and my kids. I would. I would do anything just to be close to you. I'd look after your kids. We could have more kids, whatever you wanted, wherever you wanted me."

"What, are you crazy?"

"Maybe. I just don't know how many chances in this life I am going to have for happiness, and I don't want to miss out on any of them.

There are all these things I've never said to you, and I know I'll never get the chance if I don't say it now. I would do or be anything you wanted me to be. I would like to work with you. We'd be great business partners. We'd make so much money. I'd live anywhere in the world you asked me to go."

"You're crazy. You wouldn't want to live with me."

"I am crazy. All I've thought about is you for two years, and if this is all we will ever have, this one day of passion, then that will have to be enough, but I have to tell you how I feel."

"How do you want me to answer that?"

"Of course, I want you to answer that you love me too and that you feel the same way... but I won't ask for that."

"Anne," he leaned over her and kissed me gently on the lips, "I won't be coming back to Costa Rica. You can't come to Poland. Let's not end this in sadness. No more talking." And he slid down my body and opened me up to his tongue. Licking slowly, then hungrily. I thought it couldn't happen again, I thought I was too raw, too used, but the feel of his unshaved cheeks on the inside of my thigh and the sound of his contented murmurs made me feel the languorous heat rise in me again—not fast and shaking but slowly, like a train getting up to speed, until I was arched into him and his teeth were grinding against me as I collapsed exhausted against the sheets.

And as I fell asleep, I started to try to think what time of the month it was. We hadn't used protection. Why hadn't we used protection? I'd bought condoms. They were still in my purse. It wasn't that I hadn't preferred the feel of him slick and smooth inside me, but it wasn't like me to take risks like that. I wasn't on the pill. What if, perhaps, I could keep something of him after all? I smiled at the thought.

Later, we awoke to the sound of my cell phone ringing. My car was ready. I didn't want to go. I looked back at the mess we had made of the mattress on the floor, and I wanted to climb back into the bed with him and say to hell with the world. I wanted to be a creature of passion and desire, not a woman of virtue and responsibility.

"You have to go," he said. And called me a cab. I didn't cry. I just tried to catch an image of him in my mind, an image to keep until I saw him again, whenever that may be. Perhaps a year, maybe ten, maybe never. He would always be there in my head, always be with me.

"I wish I could just be crazy and stay with you forever."

"In another life, Anne. For now you need to go home to your kids."

"I love you."

"We can't be together, but remember me."

He walked me out to the cab and gave me one last lingering kiss, then I drove away. I knew I would probably never see him again but did what I had to do—picked up my car, drove back home to my children and told no one, and went back to work.

* * *

"How did she take the news of Jimmy's death?" asked Anne's mom over the phone.

"I think she's fine," said Anne's friend Beth. "I mean, we all know she thought he was the love of her life, but it wasn't like they'd ever had a relationship."

"As her mom, I know she's been waiting for him to come back to Costa Rica. She always believed he would, that he would hate Poland and need to come back for his own sanity."

"I think it was just a crush. I mean, she should have gotten over that unrequited love thing when she was a teenager, like the rest of us. Anyway, she's fine. She went on like life was normal. Kevin told her about his death and she just did the normal things. She went to San Jose, got the car fixed, came back. I know it was probably a little shocking to hear he'd died, but..."

"His wife posted the funeral pictures today. She must have seen them on Facebook."

"She didn't mention it. She seems fine."

"You're sure she's fine? I will fly down there if I—"

"There's no need. In some ways, I think she's happier than I've seen her in a long time. Maybe now she can get on with her life. Find someone who really loves her."

"I do wish she'd stop falling for the wrong men and find someone good for her."

Chapter 5

My Father the Saint

R *eligion is mankind's greatest achievement. It shapes and molds the masses in ways they never would have thought out themselves. And often it succeeds in bettering the human condition, provided you accept its teachings, its orders, its demands. And when it fails, it is a tragedy, but not as big a tragedy as when it succeeds. For who is the bigger danger, the heretic or the saint?*

"Thank you, thank you so much." He was kissing my father's hand at the door, clutching the bread my father had given him, his face shining with the hope my father had bestowed upon him. "Thank you again, Papa."

Papa—that should be my name for him. I alone should be allowed to call him that. My father, not theirs. Yet they all called him that and he loved it. You could see it in his face. He wanted to be the father to his people, to all his people, needed and loved by all. Somehow my brother, mother and I were not enough. Our love was not enough to satisfy him. He needed to help everyone, to be loved by everyone.

I shouldn't complain. It's not that my father doesn't love me, or care for me—he does. He adores me and believes that I can do no wrong. He also believes this of my brother and everyone he meets. It's not so much that he doesn't see people's true nature, it's just that he only sees the good in all people, the true beauty in their soul, not the evil side that I can see, the ugliness that also resides in all of us right next to the beauty, the ugliness that sometimes takes control, the ugliness that is part of being human and not a saint. But my father is a saint and so he never sees that others aren't.

He calls me his devil's advocate, and it's true, but only because he's placed me in this role, the role of the realist whose job it is to try to stop the false sanctification of everyone around, the first Jewish devil's advocate, the daughter of the first Jewish saint. It was funny if you thought about it, and I did. I didn't even know who the one that was leaving was. Although he had cute eyes, dark blue with heavy lashes. I like eyes. Even without the rest of his pretty face, I would have been curious about this one. "Who was he, Father?" I'd started calling him father recently instead of papa so that I wouldn't just be one of the others, one of the many, so I could claim my place, I suppose, exert my difference.

"His name is Joshua. He's lost his job at the bank."

Of course he's lost his job. Everyone is losing their jobs; all of our people, at least. For we are the chosen few, the chosen people, the martyrs of history, but my father doesn't believe that. Doesn't believe what history tells us, doesn't believe what the Bible tells us. My father only believes the parts of the Bible that bring hope.

Sometimes I think he would have been happier as a Christian so he could read about brotherly love. As it is, he spends hours looking through the Torah and the Bible, finding those pieces he can. For his hope is in the promised land, in the future, in the promises made by an absentee God over 2000 years ago. I can't fault him for it, but I can't believe either.

"He'll be over for Passover."

Of course he would. It would be a free meal. I turned to my mother to look at her, and her face had that look it always had now. A sad resentment, another mouth she had to feed, another place she had to clean up after while my father sat, a good man, a great man, a friend to all, faithful in his observance of the Sabbath, doing nothing but reading the scriptures.

I could read her face as well as I could read his, and I wondered sometimes if he ever looked at her anymore, really looked at her. They'd been together so long I wondered if he saw her at all. She was getting thin. We all were, but she was getting thinner than the rest of us because it was she who went without when there was no more. That piece of bread that left tonight with handsome Joshua would have been her share.

I would try to give her some of mine to sop up the thin soup, but she would smile and push it back at me, then try to tell me halfway through her soup that she'd had enough and would I like the rest? I would refuse, as always, but my brother never understood that this was just a game one played, and, selfish by nature, would say that he would eat it. So he would take it from her, then eat his own and hers. It was the same almost every night. And since we could only shop at the Jewish stores now, there was so little to buy even if one had extra money, which we never did.

My father should have been a rabbi. It would have suited his temperament and life. Actually, I often think he would have been best born a Catholic and become a monk so that he could love mankind and help them freely without the encumbrance of a family. But rather than become a rabbi, his mother had insisted he grow up to be a silversmith as his father and grandfather before him.

When I was born, we were wealthy. My father was known far and wide for his beautiful craftsmanship and he was a hard worker, but even without the Nazis and their restrictions on occupations, my father would have been poor by now. His eyesight was deteriorating even when I was a child. He needed thicker and thicker glasses and could not see to do fine work. And he never made a good business decision.

There was his first business partner, who stole his business name and location, then the employee he had when I was a baby who stole all the silver in the shop one evening, then the other employee whom my father trained and sponsored who left with half my father's clients to go to the opposition. And these were just the highlights. My father never spoke badly of these men and never went after any of them for what was owed to him. Stealing from my father was just one more way to get ahead in Dusseldorf, probably listed in the local guidebook.

The last argument I had heard my parents have was about one of these men. "Josef, you need to fire Stephano. You know silver is disappearing. He's the only one but you who has access to the safe."

"Annegret, you worry too much. I am sure that Stephano must just have put extra silver into the last piece he did. I'll make sure he doesn't on the next one. He's only learning, you know..."

"I know, but one gram here, another there... We don't have the—"

"This is my business, Annegret. I am the man. I will deal with it."

For, of course, Stephano could not be a thief. My father, who could never believe that anyone was evil, was always willing to vilify my mother in order to stop her from telling him the truth. For my mother was the only one he ever believed could be wrong. And three months later when Stephano quit, taking the entire contents of the safe with him, cash and silver, my mother could never say "I told you so," because my father would need comforting. He would cry and weep in dismay that he had been so badly betrayed and it was so unexpected. And my mother would get thinner eating only her own anger.

Seder was thirty-six people that week. Some of them had brought things and my mother managed to make soup and bake bread. There wouldn't be a lot, but everyone would have something, even if it was just a thin soup with a tiny matzo ball in it and a piece of matzah bread.

Joshua was there, and as I had thought, he was pretty, possibly even beautiful. He sat next to me at the table, wedging his way in. I felt both flattered and frightened. My stomach clenched into a knot and I poured most of my soup into my mother's bowl while she was out finding glasses for everyone. "Hello. I saw you the other day."

"Yes, I saw you too." I found myself looking into his eyes, then lowered my head, blushing.

"Your father is a great man." Oh, not this conversation. I didn't want to talk about my father. I didn't want to hear how great he was, how he helped everyone and how he was such a wonderful leader, friend, savior, mensch. The conversation I wanted to have went, "You are so beautiful. Would you come out with me?" "It must be wonderful having such a man as a father."

"Sure. People say I look like him."

"You do. It's in the warmth of your lovely eyes." Well, this was sounding a little better, the warmth of my eyes. It was a pathetic line but if that was as good as he could do... I batted them slightly and hoped he would continue. "If I'm not too bold and if you are available—"

"I am available for anything." If only he knew how true that was. Being the daughter of a saint was an exhausting job. I was expected by all, including my father, to be good and pure and sweet and virtuous. The expectation had created the reality. I had to live in the purified air of my father's sanctity.

He stopped for a second, taken back, then shook it off, convincing himself I did not mean any innuendo. "Then if you would like to accompany me Monday evening to a Kulturbund performance?"

I nodded. A date. A chance to get out of the house. My parents wouldn't let me out in the evening on my own anymore. Not since we'd started wearing the armbands. The last time I'd gone out on my own, a man had spat on me. I recognized him but he no longer knew me. I wasn't a person, just a Jew. The armband had changed my status from person to object.

"I'll ask your father if you can go."

Of course. Of course he couldn't be man enough to just sweep me off my feet and take me out for the evening. I looked at him from the side as he asked my father's permission. He had such lovely bones; I wanted to run my finger along his jawline next to where already his shave was starting to fail and the prickly manliness of his beard was reappearing next to his side curls.

My father looked at me, then at my mother for approval, then nodded. I could go out with Joshua. I wanted to laugh. Instead I passed the salt down the table and took another mouthful of soup.

Monday came slowly, as all days that one waits for do. And at last he was there and we were off. My father was busy helping a married couple settle a dispute, but my mother bade me be careful as we went out into the dusk.

Joshua took my hand. His was warm and dry. I leaned against him, pretending I was cold, and he put his arm around me. It felt good, it felt right, and for once I was just myself. When we reached the shadows of the theater, I got up on my toes and kissed him gently on the lips.

He kissed me back and I remember nothing about the show we saw. I know it wasn't Beethoven or Wagner, for German music was banned in a Jewish theater, but what it was exactly I will never remember.

Later I would complain to him that I should have watched the show instead of staring into his eyes, because it was the last show we saw together. The theater was closed down and there was no entertainment to go to at all. So now our evenings were sitting on my parents' settee.

He came often enough that it was obvious to all how he felt about me, and I loved having him as a boyfriend. We took long walks with stolen kisses, and finally he got up the courage to ask my father for my hand. I would have liked him to ask me first, but...

The golden halo of my first love could not disguise the ugliness around us. My father met day and night with other old men. From the pieces I heard, it was obvious that life was becoming harder and harder for our people.

My brother was sent home from school. Jewish children were no longer welcome in class, so our living room became an elementary school. Joshua became the teacher for the boy. I helped out the girls. Working with him in such close confines filled me with impure thoughts. All I wanted to do was be alone with him, but there were always too many people around. Even when class was finally dismissed, he would run to my father to tell him about his day.

And I wondered if Joshua loved me, or whether he loved my father and I was just a vehicle to get closer to him.

My mother pulled me aside one day as the men sat talking Torah and solving the problems of the world in the living room.

"Come, Greta, help me in the kitchen." I followed dutifully, knowing there was nothing in the kitchen my mother did not have under control and nothing much to cook, anyway. She put a spoon in my hand and stationed me at the soup pot while she proceeded to dice onions.

"Stir," she said. "You know, no matter how little else you have in the soup, so long as there are plenty of onions, everyone feels like they ate well."

"Yes, Mother."

She scraped one lot of onions in, then went back to the rest. Then her hands stopped. I looked at her and it looked like there were tears in her eyes. They must have been terribly strong onions. "I am worried."

"Yes..." Was my mother worried about Joshua and me? I didn't think I had let my feelings show. We were engaged now, and I hadn't touched him in front of the children, although I'd wanted to.

"The word has come that we are all about to move. Your father thinks it is wonderful. He'll tell you all about it this evening, how we are finally going to the promised land away from the hatred of the Nazis, the dislike of the Germans."

"But you don't, Mamma?"

"I have a bad feeling in my heart, daughter, and I need your promise." She took my hands from the spoon and it fell down into the thin soup. "Promise me. If I can get you passage out, you will leave."

"Without you?"

"Without all of us, without even Joshua. Promise me."

She was looking at me and I could see that her eyes were really crying, not just onions. A drop slid down her hollowed-out cheek and into the soup pot. I couldn't say no, not when she asked like that. I nodded. She nodded back and started cutting the next onion.

I stirred the pot. Leave without Joshua, without them. For where? Why would she ask such a thing of me? If everyone was going to the promised land, why was it that I could not follow?

At dinner, Father broke the news that Mother had already told me. "It will be wonderful, daughter, a land of our own. The Germans don't want us and we will have peace. Just Jews, free to live like we wish, with all our own traditions and laws."

"It sounds wonderful," said Joshua, answering something that had been directed at me. He'd been doing that more and more of late, and this time I didn't find it cute.

"Yes, Father," I said, and there looking across the table straight at me was my mother, the woman who had not cried as my father had given away everything we once had, the woman who had borne nine children only to see all but two die. And I'd been there for the last birth. She'd not cried even then, but today, today she'd cried and I had promised. "When do we leave?"

"In a couple of weeks, they'll bring train cars for us all and we'll ride out. We need to start packing up all our things. I'll be in charge of making sure everyone on our block is ready in time."

So that meant my mother and I would be doing all the actual work of packing our family. It was as it always was, and I pulled my lips into a smile for my mother and lowered my head. I would do as I had promised. I was a dutiful daughter, and she had gotten my agreement first.

While Father bustled around the neighborhood helping everyone pack and sell their favorite things, Mother and I prepared our household. From the floorboards of her room, she pulled out some beautiful silver and gold pieces.

"These were your grandfather's washing cup, and your grandmother's jewelry," she explained, and I looked at her emaciated frame and wondered at a will that could keep such luxuries while denying herself food. "I have found a man who can get you out of here. Take the cup, and this necklace. They are emeralds. Break it up slowly and it should be enough money for your new life. The rest will need to be sold to pay for your passport and passage."

"Where am I to go?"

"America, until all this is over." But she said it with such finality, as if she didn't believe it would ever be over. "It is all arranged. You leave the same day they pack the trains. I will tell your father and Joshua you missed our train and caught the next. Just stay here in the house and a man called Mikal will come."

"Shouldn't you send Jacob? He is your son."

"He won't want to leave his father. He's not strong enough to be alone. You are."

"How will I know where you have gone?" I asked her.

"I know where you will be, my dear, and I will contact you."

I nodded and stared at the jewelry and riches at our feet. I picked up the pieces she wanted me to take with me. "Won't you need some of these, Mother?"

She shook her head and sighed. "Now sew those into your clothes so no one finds them."

The day came quickly. Joshua and my father were in heaven, excited. They hurried pulling our things out to the station then going back to help others with theirs. My brother was complaining about having to carry too much, although he carried the same as our mother.

"Your father is a great man, Greta. You know, he helped arrange for this to happen. I mean, some people said we couldn't trust the Germans, but your father talked them around. And now look." I looked out at the sea of faces, most of them trusting and happy, some of them, like my mother, scared and stoney. All of them sitting on their luggage, waiting in lines, waiting for the train cars. The luxury train cars to take them to the promised land. Finally, up pulled a train towing cattle cars.

"Papa," Joshua turned to my father, confused, "where are the luxury train cars?"

"They must all be at the front, taking soldiers to war. Come, let's not dawdle. We don't want to miss the train."

"But what about the luggage?"

My father worked his way towards the front to talk to a guard, then he smiled and addressed the crowd. "People, do not worry. This is the correct train. The passenger train was derailed by the enemy. Your luggage will be loaded on separately. Everyone, just make sure your boxes are marked with your name and proceed in an orderly single-file fashion into the boxcars. We will soon be at our new home, Dachau."

There was a cheer, and everyone started to enter just as my father had told them to. While he stood benevolently like a host, welcoming them all aboard.

"Greta." My mother nodded at me and handed me the bag we knew was my things to go to America with. "Joshua, I have forgotten something. Greta, can you please go home and get it for me?"

"But what if she misses the train?" Joshua said, not even looking at me or her, just at my father.

"Then I'm sure in the end we will all be in the same place," I said, annoyed with him, annoyed that he wasn't going to see me leave, wasn't going to say goodbye, wasn't going to kiss me one last time.

"Well, I'll go help your father."

"No," said my mother and grabbed his arm as he went to leave. "Give her a kiss for luck, so that she makes it on the train."

He looked embarrassed but turned to kiss me. I threw my arms around him and gave him the kiss I had been saving for our wedding day, saving forever. A kiss to say goodbye and hello and all the things I could never say. He pulled out of my arms, reddened and shocked.

"I must go," he said and ran to my father.

"Of course, you must," I said. "Goodbye," I said when he was too far into the crowd to hear.

I turned back to my mother. "Thank you."

"Look after yourself, child, and whatever you think later, know that your parents loved you." She kissed me on the cheek and turned to go. "Goodbye."

"Goodbye," I called after her and she disappeared into the crowd, a thin stick of a woman disappearing into a sea of heavy clothing.

I turned back to the apartment. Mikal met me as the trains pulled out of the station.

And later, when I thought back on it all, I tried not to hate my father. And when he was the only one who survived, the good man who'd helped everyone, even selecting his own wife for the ovens in order to save another, I would repeat her words to myself, "know that your parents loved you."

Chapter 6

The Tigers Come at Night

We live in the light, enjoying our days, working, playing, resting, loving. But when the sun fades and night brings the hidden fears and dangers, we huddle around our fires, listening to sounds in the dark, to the creatures that stalk us, waiting to take us even in our dreams.

I look normal. Well, maybe not normal. There are not so many 6'4" 240-pound men walking around. I'm a big guy. But that's what Sandra liked about me. Normal enough; you couldn't tell by looking at me. I seem just like everyone else.

Sandra was 5'4", 140 pounds, well-proportioned if you know what I mean. She thought she was fat. I thought she was perfect. We married just out of college, and I won't say I never looked at another woman, but when I got home she was everything I needed. I never regretted a single day married to her. I just wish I'd been a better husband, a better man for her. I wish that every time she cried, I'd understood instead of just leaving her alone. I wish... I wish so many things. Regret is all I have now. It's all my fault, everything. Not just her death. I mean everything. It's all my fault.

We had a happy marriage. She loved me, too. Really loved me, despite my faults. Despite everything. The first time it happened, she understood. She knew I wasn't awake. She'd seen me sleepwalk often enough. I think the sleep apnea made it worse, and the weight gain. I mean, I've been trying to lose weight. I was 270. At 200 I'm a stick man. I mean, I'm a big guy so 240 isn't that big for me. She liked that I was so big. As if that meant I could protect her and make her feel safe. She was so wrong.

She used to say that I made her feel like a dainty fairy. When I held her, she felt dainty. I could easily pick her up. When I look at photos of us at the wedding, she looks like a child, so young. And even last year at our 25th anniversary, she still looked like a doll, like a beautiful china doll. Oh my God, so fragile.

I was never good enough for her. Oh my God, but I loved her. You need to believe me. I loved her so much.

The first time I heard screaming in the night I got up and turned on the light. She sat up in bed. Coughing. She had her hands to her neck.

I asked her what was wrong. She answered very calmly that I had been strangling her in my sleep. She pulled her hands back and I could see the red marks my hands had made around her throat. That was the first night she went to sleep in the guest room. After a couple of days, she'd moved back in. Then last year I had a nightmare that there were robbers in the house. I got up to look around in my dream and she got up to see what was wrong.

I thought she was a robber, and I hit her. Like really hit her, and I broke her nose. Her screaming woke me up again that time. She was on the floor, holding her face. I took her to the hospital.

Yes, I am sure you have the police report. She explained it then. To everyone. My doctor sent in a report too. Sent me to another sleep study. Ordered me a new CPAP machine because I had thrown the last one and shattered it. This time the diagnosis was night terrors. Some kind of switch in my brain doesn't shut off so I act out my dreams. It's not funny. This last year I have punched through two windows trying to get out of my bedroom. I broke the door a month ago and had to get a carpenter in. I don't know why Sandra stayed with me. I really don't. I mean, I know she says she loves me, but... I mean, she said she loved me. I don't know how to... how to explain. I can't believe she's dead. I should be dead; she should be here. She'd know how to explain it all. She'd know what to say.

Anyway, I got seventeen stitches in this hand. See, here, through the thumb. That was from when I punched out a mirror in the bedroom. Finally, she had no choice. She stopped sleeping with me. She locked me in every night, and locked herself in. We put a piece of plywood across the inside of the window the last time I punched it out. I mean, we got it fixed—the neighbors don't need to ask why we don't fix our windows—but after it was fixed, I screwed up a piece of plywood. Sandra insisted on painting the board so it looked like curtains, but I'm not sure it fooled anybody. And of course, the mirrors all got taken out of the room, and the furniture except the bed, and I couldn't even take in a glass of water.

Yep, I couldn't even have a glass of water. See this scar across my palm? I woke up one night soaking wet and found out that I'd crushed a glass of water in my sleep. Crushed it in my hand. The bed was wet with water and blood, and I was covered with little glass shards. I don't even know how I did it. I don't think I could consciously crush a glass in my hand. Even if I wanted to, even if I could turn off the fear of the shards of glass. Shards of glass the doctor needed to pull out with tweezers slowly for about an hour. Some cuts were too small for stitches—all the little glue dots that kept my hand together while it healed. And repainting the door from all the blood spots as I beat on it to wake her up. So, no more drinks in the bedroom.

I thought we'd fixed all the possibilities. And then my mom died. And we came out here, to her house, to clean up and get it ready to sell. My mom told me I'd been sleepwalking my whole life, but that most of the time I'd go to her room and we'd discuss the weather and the football and she'd walk me back to my own bed. Tonight I dreamed about my mom. My mom and the tigers.

In my sleep my mom was alive. She came to my room and told me that tigers had escaped the zoo and were in the house. I got up and walked into the kitchen with her. A huge tiger jumped on her, and I grabbed a kitchen knife and stabbed, slashed out at the tiger. It jumped on me and I stabbed up at it. That was when I woke up.

And saw all this and called you.

The cop looked down at me, still sitting in the middle of the kitchen in a pool of Sandra's blood, and handed me a paper towel for my tears.

Chapter 7

Getting it Right

"*Two roads diverged in a wood...*" *Perhaps the most important words in the English language. The choices we make, in every aspect of life, that make us who we are, what we accomplish, and perhaps most importantly the effect we have on others. We are given choices, and when we refuse to accept that gift we let the future fall to others.*

We can make mistakes and fail, but what if we could correct the mistakes...

Stephanie knew the minute she saw the television in Sears. The face was repeated in the sea of sets. A face familiar, almost identical, with long, dark wavy hair, large deep-set brown eyes hidden behind thick glasses. This woman on the television was thinner, of course. She wasn't carrying the weight of four pregnancies, the softness under the chin, over the arms, thighs and entire body. But the mole, the one by her lip, was there. It was the face Stephanie saw in the mirror, yet it wasn't her.

Stephanie reached for the television screen with her left hand while her right hand unconsciously went to her own mole, a brown hairy thing that her father had called her beauty spot and the kids at school had called her pet. It had been weeks since she'd looked in a mirror, or used her tweezers, and her fingers played with the hairs.She looked around. The other televisions repeating the image. She pulled open the panel and turned up the sound; she leaned in close to hear it over the music coming from the nearby stereos. "... my office is disappointed by the judge's decision, but we still have enough evidence to prosecute this case." The woman's name popped up on the screens: Jennifer Litton–Assistant District Attorney. The picture changed to the mug shot of the accused, another decrepit used-to-be celebrity enjoying another fifteen minutes of fame at the expense of his decapitated wife.Stephanie started to flick channels to see if any other channel had the picture of Jennifer.

Stephanie wanted to see her hands, to see if she was wearing a ring. Stephanie touched her left hand, reaching for the white, withered flesh on her ring finger, the scar of ten years.

She found her face again on the E Channel. In the moments of flicking, Stephanie had convinced herself she was wrong, but then she saw the footage again. This woman, Jennifer, was here. A different her, the woman she could have been, the woman she had wanted to be once, before she'd met Simon, before her dreams had been co-opted to wife and mother. This woman was whom she was going to be when she grew up, before when all that mattered was grades and exams, before love, before the miscarriages, before regret.

In a moment of clarity, Stephanie knew in exactly which moment her life had failed. The one thing she could change, and it would all be different. It wasn't a big moment, not one of the ones she had agonized over. It wasn't when she'd said yes to his proposal or even when she'd taken the job so they could buy a house instead of going back to college. The exact moment was when she was ten. The day she had picked up the fliers about summer camp. The day she'd decided to go to Science Camp, not the camp at the lake.

If she'd never gone to that camp, her life would have been different. In the past, she'd always blamed herself for going with the camp counselor to his office. Blamed herself for not screaming when he approached her. Blamed herself for letting him kiss her, hated herself for responding when he touched her. Without camp, she wouldn't have needed Simon, wouldn't have become Stephanie. She would have lived out her dreams, become Jennifer.

And in that moment of clarity, she stopped blaming herself. Her fate was sealed the day she picked up the camp flier. Stephanie had thought all the other fates were murdered that day by an insignificant action, but seeing Jennifer she knew it wasn't so.

The other woman on the television set was her. Her with another fate. Maybe somewhere out there another version of her was living out that other life she had wanted. Maybe somewhere out there was the wife and mother she had wanted to be. Perhaps somewhere out there she was getting her life right, living out the other fates, whereas somehow she herself had walked into the cloakroom of life and collected the wrong one.

"Can I help you, ma'am?"

She turned, startled. He looked too young to be working. She wondered for a minute what he would be like to kiss. Would his skin still have a soft downiness or by morning would the stubble on his jaw run like sandpaper across her breasts? He had wide shoulders—probably a surfer—with corded arms and a contoured torso. She looked back at his face and his eyes. In his eyes, she felt his lack of interest. She was a mom type, possibly one of his mom's friends. Was she that old? Was she really old enough to be his mother? Oh, God, maybe she was. When had she gotten so old?

"Are you interested in a TV? If you apply for a Sears's card today, you can get 10% off your first purchase."

"No, thanks," she smiled. "Could you tell me where the firearms are?"

"Second floor, sporting goods, behind the treadmills."

"Thank you." She walked towards the elevator to buy her gun. Her fate had been decided long before. There was the comfort that somewhere out there it didn't have to end like this. Somewhere another her, with a different name, had collected one of the other fates and was getting her life right.

Chapter 8

Dark Man

The world used to be black and white, and then it got co-opted. Now it is dark and light, darkness no longer confined to the night, but growing in every shadow, for the shadows themselves have grown more opaque. Things hide in the shadows, things dangerous and evil, things it is madness to oppose. You can only run for the light. If you can run fast enough.

Jessica drove the minivan cautiously up the long gravel driveway. The vehicle lurched in the potholes its headlights could not illuminate. She moved the rearview mirror so she could see David, still sleeping in his car seat despite the last pothole. Adjusting the mirror again, she saw the figure of a man. He was moving towards her, a shape growing larger in the glow of her taillights. It must be a shadow, she thought. There couldn't be anyone here—not here.

She wondered for a moment whether he was a worker from the new development down the road. Someone lost. Their house was set on the edge of the city, an old farmhouse on a half-acre of land. The rest of the farm was slowly being turned into tract housing. She looked in the mirror again. The man was not walking yet seemed to be just drifting closer. She started to turn her head to look at him directly, then she stopped. She watched her mirror again. She was filled with a new awareness, a certain terror. She knew that if she turned to look, he would not be there. In that instant, she knew this person in her mirror was not a construction worker.

She kept driving, and he kept approaching. Reaching the end of the driveway, she pulled right up to the wooden fence. She couldn't outrun him; there was nowhere left to run. Looking in the mirror, she knew she had to turn, see with her own eyes. She dropped her key into its usual place in the car. Then she turned in her seat and looked back through the rear window; there was no one there. She pushed herself away from the rearview mirror and out of the car. The night was cold and still. She could hear her own terror as she opened the rear door and jerked her son from his car seat and into her arms. Hurrying towards the porch light, she resisted looking back, for she knew she would see nothing. But she could feel him watching her, feel the shadow of his soul in her mind.

The sanctuary of the porch light beckoned. She ran, her lungs aching. Sir William, her Siamese cat, was sitting on the porch waiting for her. He stood up to greet her with a long yowl. Reaching the light, she stood leaning on the house and stilled her breath. There was nothing to be afraid of. It had just been a shadow; couldn't be anything else. Holding David with one arm, she opened the door and let herself and the cat in.

Harry had come home and fed himself. Spaghetti sauce was burning on the stove. She laid David on his bed and ran back to the kitchen to turn it off. "Hi, baby," he said, coming into the kitchen, pushing aside her long hair and kissing her on the neck. "How was your mom?"

"Harry, have you noticed anything strange?""I've always thought your mom was strange. Hey, you look white and exhausted; it must be all that driving."

"Yes. I must be tired. That must be it." It had been nothing. Here in the light she was convinced; it was just a shadow, a trick of the light, an image burned into her tired retina from days before. There had been no one following her.

"Do you want me to make you something?"

"No, I think I'll just go to bed and watch TV."

He smiled at her. "I think I'll join you. Maybe I can even get you in the mood for something other than TV."

* * *

When they had moved into the two-bedroom house, they had easily fit all of the furniture that had formerly filled their one-bedroom apartment in the city. This was their dream house, away from the noise, with plenty of room for a garden. A safe place to raise a family. Yes, there had been compromises. The house was smaller than she could have wished, and when they moved in it needed a lot of work. Every weekend for the first year, they painted, patched, or planted. When she became pregnant, the cozy house was suddenly tiny.

Harry had built her a room in the garage when David was a baby, an office so she could still work from home part-time. It was her space, with lilac walls, Monet prints, lace curtains, and flowery upholstery, feminine touches she would never have forced on Harry. They'd put in a big picture window so she could look up from whatever tax return she was working on and see David playing in the yard. She usually worked there every morning, but since she had come home from her mother's, she just stayed in the house, keeping David close. He seemed happy enough, a little tired after the trip, but what could you expect from a five-year-old? Visiting Grandma had taken a lot out of both of them. That's all that is wrong, she told herself—exhaustion, and a hangover from being pleasant to Mother.

David had been spoiled by his grandma: candy and ice cream, presents every day. Jessica had tried to stop her mother, but it had only been for three days after all. Now back home, David demanded the royal treatment he had received from Grandma. "Give me candy."

"No, David," she said, looking up from the sauce she was stirring. Tonight would be homemade Salisbury steak, Harry's favorite, and macaroni and cheese for David.

"Oh, why not?" He hit the ground crying.

"Because it's not good food, that's why. I'm making dinner right now."

Harry walked in from work as David whined out his best argument and then started sobbing.

"Grandma would let me have candy. You don't love me."

"Oh Christ, Jessica," said Harry, looking down at his son. "Don't tell me you've let your mother wreck our kid and turn him into a little monster. David, get off your knees." David started to sob louder. Jessica bent down and got on the floor with her son. "Hey, Davy-do," she said, pulling up his shirt, "if you don't stop crying I'm going to have to tickle you until you pee."

"Mama..."

She blew a raspberry into his bellybutton, and he started to giggle. "Now get up and bring your daddy that picture you were drawing, pronto. Dinner will be on the table in ten." David ran off to get the picture.

"Jessica, did you let your mom jack him up on sugar while..."

"Harry, she doesn't see him often."

"She shouldn't see him at all if that is what..."

"It'll be ok." She put her arms around his waist. "So, how was your day?"

"Good. Did you get a chance to look at all the mail that came in while you were gone? I think I saw some envelopes that looked like they might contain checks."

Jessica put the plates out on the small table in the kitchen where they usually ate. "No, I didn't have a chance yet."

"Well, it's all waiting for you in your office. If there are any checks, it could really help out; the property tax is due this week." Harry set the cutlery out while Jessica started dishing the food.

"Daddy!" yelled David as he ran back into the kitchen. He laid his picture on the table. Harry looked down at the stick people and swirling colors.

"Tell me about it, kiddo."

David started to point. "Well, that's you, me, Mommy, and the house, and there is the Dark Man behind us and it's raining and..."

Jessica stopped. "What man, honey?"

"That one, and there's a storm, 'cause of clouds. When is it going to snow?"

"It doesn't snow here," said Harry.

"Marti at school says snow is like ice cream. Can you eat it?"

"Sit at the table, kiddo, and let's eat. Mom has made a great meal. Snow is more like ice than ice cream—it doesn't taste sweet."

Harry laid the cutlery out on the table and started to serve. He grinned at Jessica as he put three Salisbury steaks on his own plate.

"Wow! Marti wrong. Can we make a snowman?" "Sure, Davey. When we go to the snow we can." Everyone sat and started to eat. There was never any prayer or ceremony. The only dinner rule Jessica had ever insisted on was that the television must be off. "Hey, Jessica, are you ok? You aren't eating."

"Yeah, I'm fine." She forced in a mouthful. There was nothing wrong; David's picture was just a few scribbles on a piece of paper. For all she knew, she had given him the idea of the Dark Man. There was nothing to be afraid of, yet she had to force herself to eat.

Jessica spent the next morning opening mail and filing. Two clients had paid their bills and there was money to deposit, so she readied the banking, then went back into the house to make a cup of coffee.

David was at school and Harry was at work; the house was silent. Sir William met her as she walked up to it. He was lonely. He rubbed himself against her legs as she entered the house, and stood talking to her as she made the coffee. She reached down to pat him and, acknowledged, he walked to the bedroom to catch some more sleep.

Jessica walked back to her office and went to turn the handle. The door was jammed. The handle wouldn't move. She rotated her wrist, and her hand slid around. It felt as if someone were holding it on the other side, preventing it from turning. Jessica put down her coffee and tried the handle again with both hands. It turned easily, but the door opened slowly, as if someone were pushing back against her. Then the door sprang open. She looked inside the office; it was just as she had left it. She looked behind the door, but she could see no one.

She tried the handle; it moved easily. She pushed the door back and forth; it moved freely. She ran around the building. Looking down the driveway, it was empty. She told herself the door had just frozen, then freed itself; happens all the time. There had to be a reasonable explanation. Taking the banking from the desk, she ran back to the house, curled up on the bed and grabbed the cat for comfort.

* * *

Jessica was sorting laundry when she heard a door open behind her. She turned from the washer and saw the living room door open.

Sir William's paw appeared, then he walked through. Jessica sighed, realizing she had been holding her breath. It was only the cat.

There was nothing wrong. It was all in her head. She bit her lip and wondered what was happening to her. Perhaps this feeling that there was someone in the house was a manifestation of her fear of being alone. Perhaps she was just worried because David was at school now and the house was empty. She never used to jump when the cat came into the room. It was all in her head. No need to worry anyone else; it was all in her head. She really wanted to believe it was all in her head.

She took an armful of clothes into David's room. She and David had painted the room together—blue with taupe accents. A job that would have taken her two days had taken the two of them a week. She looked at the wall where she could still see his handprints; the paint hadn't quite covered the mistakes. Walking up, she traced the marks with her finger. His hands were so small.

As she put the clothes away, she saw the mouse ears. They were David's prize possession, proof of their vacation to Disneyworld. Harry had come home from work with a surprise. He had gotten a bonus and had spent the money on a trip for the three of them to Disneyworld. Jessica half-wished he had spent the money on a trip somewhere romantic for just the two of them. Harry was a great father and provider, but she missed the tender lover she had married.

* * *

It was 2 a.m. when Jessica awoke. She pulled the blankets up but couldn't get warm. David was asleep between Harry and herself again; he had climbed into bed without waking her up this time.

For the last few weeks, she had to lie down with him in his room to get him to sleep. He wouldn't let her turn the light out because he said he was scared. He used to go to sleep alone in the dark and now she had to lie with him or he would cry. The precious free time she got after

David went to bed was being eaten away. He would clutch onto her for an hour, and then, when she tried to leave, he would wake up and cling to her again. She would lie with him in the dark, slowly resenting his dependence.

"All kids go through this phase," Harry assured her. Yet he was never the one who had to put Davey to sleep. He didn't have to hold the shaking, exhausted little boy until his arms went numb all the time, knowing that the dishes were waiting to be done in the kitchen.

Jessica rubbed the sleep out of her eyes. There was something coming into the room. She reached for David, protective, scared. The door opened. It was Sir William, who walked over to the foot of the bed. Then he stood still. The cat's back arched and his hair stood on end and he was glaring at the corner of the room above the dresser.

David moaned in his sleep and tossed the covers off. Jessica put them back on, but he started to yell. He was drenched with sweat. His hands clawed the air above him. "No, no, no, leave me alone, leave me alone!" His legs kicked out wildly. The cat began to yowl.

Harry woke up. "What the hell? Shut that cat up. It's waking up David."

David's eyes opened, unseeing.

"NO, NO, NO!" yelled David.

"JESSICA, do something to that cat." The cat began to howl louder.

David's arms started to fly; one hit her in the face. "LEAVE ME ALONE", he screamed.

"If you don't stop that damn cat, I will."

Jessica hopped out of bed and picked up the spitting ball of fur. The cat continued to hiss at something in the corner of the room. She could almost see, there in the corner, the Dark Man the cat could sense.

"Get out of here!" she yelled at the shadow. The cat hurled himself from her arms and ran out of the room. David calmed immediately, and Harry put his arms around him.

"It's ok, kiddo. Go back to sleep."

Jessica couldn't shut her eyes again that night. As a child, she had believed that her dolly could place a protective field around her as she went to sleep. Now, in her desperation, she imagined a white sheet of light surrounding their bed, a bubble of protection. She held David tight, his cold skin sticking to hers. She watched the darkness for the unseen enemy and she listened to her baby breathing.

* * *

It was a beautiful Saturday, and they were out in the yard. The orange tree they had planted when they first moved in was covered in fruit. Fat squirrels ran along the phone wires, playing tag.

Harry and David played ball while Jessica read a romance novel and watched. Sir William had joined the family and lounged in the sun by the fence. Then Harry threw the ball hard. The ball hit David on the forehead. Falling backward against the house wall, he sank to the ground, stunned and weeping.

Jessica jumped out of her deck chair to run to him. Harry stood in front of her and held her back. "He didn't get hurt that bad. Don't spoil him. You'll make him into a sissy."

David's body reverberated with pain.

"Get out of the way, Harry!" she yelled and pushed against him.

"You'll just spoil the boy, ruin him. Let him cry; it'll teach him." Harry's hand caught her arm. His fingers cut deep into her flesh.

Sir William ran next to David and started to howl blood-curdling, anguished cries, his body swollen like a puffer fish.

She looked back at Harry, and for a moment she didn't recognize him. His face had changed. How couldn't she identify him? He was the man she loved, the man she had lived with for ten years. She knew every line in his face, every mood reflected in his eyes. In a crowded room, she knew him just from a glimpse of the back of his head. Why couldn't she recognize him? What was going on?

"No! Go away, go away, go away!" screamed David.

The cat started to spit at Harry. Jessica stared down at Sir William. What was wrong with their cat? What had happened to Harry? Suddenly she understood. This wasn't her husband. The Dark Man had caught up to them. It wasn't her imagination. Looking at the stranger looking out of her husband's eyes, she knew this was real, and it was too late. She did the only thing she could.

She grabbed David and ran for the car.

Harry started after her. She couldn't run fast carrying David. He was gaining on her. She could feel his fingertips grabbing at the back of her shirt.

"Fucking beast!" He let go, and she looked to see Sir William jump up and attack Harry's face.

The key was in the car where she always left it and, as she accelerated down the driveway, she didn't look back.

Chapter 9

Slip-Sliding Away

*O*ur minds and memory are necessary, vital, the essence of who we are. Necessary, so we forgive them when they play tricks on us. Forget this, misplace that. I was sure I paid that bill. I've never seen that building before. But what if you were seeing another choice, another possibility, another timeline that you couldn't justify? What if you were slip-sliding away?

Two o'clock Friday afternoon, Susan went to walk home the way she always did. Out the door of her office, across Sunset Blvd, past the old Home Savings Bank Building and up Vine to the subway station at Hollywood and Vine, Red Line to North Hollywood, then a block to her apartment. As she walked past the Home Savings Bank building—it was a Chase now, she reminded herself—she almost walked into a huge fountain with a statue in it. Now, walking into things was not unusual for Susan. She was notably clumsy, even compared to other people who passed their days staring at computer screens doing accounting and having their minds destroyed by QuickBooks. The thing was, Susan had never seen this statue before. As someone who had worked in the same building and walked the same route home every day for twenty years, this was surprising.

Susan walked around the fountain. It was spraying water up around a large, rather obscene statue of a naked woman riding a bull backwards while a flying cherub was strangling her. Susan stared at the statue. She looked over at the building. It looked the same as it always had, with its large tile murals on the outside. It was a low but beautiful building, too pretty to be a bank, a white decorated candy box of a building surrounded by glass and metal skyscrapers. But this fountain... how long had this fountain been there? She shook her head. She was obviously going crazy. There was no way the fountain had just appeared. Obviously, she just hadn't noticed it before. She put her head down and marched herself to the train and got off in NoHo at the end of the line. The statue bothered her, and she googled it; it was a copy of a statue called *The Flight of Europa* made by someone called Paul Manship. She'd never heard of him, but it seemed so horribly inappropriate of a thing to put in front of a bank. A statue of Zeus as a bull kidnapping Europa so he could rape her. Only men could find art in rape. She shook her head, put on her pajamas, picked up her latest romance novel, and went to bed.

Monday morning, she decided to walk down the other side of Vine Street. It wasn't a conscious decision, just the kind of thing someone does when they don't want to think about the enormous statue that arrived in the middle of their normal walk path. And she kept telling herself, because she was a sensible woman, it had always been there; the internet said it had been there since 1969 so it was just somehow that she'd never seen it. How she'd never seen it she didn't know, but obviously it was so, for the statue was there.

She walked past the Ricardo Montalban theater. She remembered the first time she'd run into a celebrity. She'd been in a hurry from the bus to work. There was no train in those days and the bus was running late, so she wasn't looking where she was going. She hadn't been in Los Angeles long, and she'd never seen a celebrity. And she ran straight into him. Straight into Ricardo Montalban and knocked off his walking stick to the ground. She was of the generation that grew up watching television after school and she felt so guilty and also excited to see Mr. Rourke from *Fantasy Island* twisted around her feet on the ground. She helped him up. "I'm so sorry. I'm so sorry, I didn't mean to—"

He responded in his polished-silver voice, "It's fine, no problem at all."

And she'd blushed. Then, seeing him back on his feet, she'd run to work, still afraid of being late. Still afraid of being fired. Barry used to stand by the elevators back then, counting down. Twelve minutes was as late as you could be by Californian law, and everyone who walked in thirteen minutes late was fired. Barry was not a mean man, just following the boss's orders.

The theater hadn't been called the Montalban Theater then; she doesn't know what it was called. He must have bought it soon before or after she ran him over. Funny, she'd heard he'd died after finally ending up in a wheelchair. She hoped she hadn't contributed to that. Reaching down, she touched her knee. It was tender. She didn't know exactly what she'd done, but she was noticing it now—a dull aching deep inside the knee that turned into a stabbing sharpness when she went to kneel down. She'd thought when she first felt it that she had banged her knee on something—she was always banging herself on something—but then when it hadn't turned blue, or red, or green, or any of the colors she associated with a bruise she realized the damage was deeper. Deep inside, somewhere in her knee, she had broken something. This is what happens when you pass fifty, she told herself and tried not to think how much she would hurt by the time she hit seventy, or God forbid, eighty-two like her own mother.

When she got to the corner, she looked over across the street and there was the fountain. And in her mind, she could see that it had always been there, and in her mind she remembered it arriving yesterday. And she felt scared, as if somehow everything was slipping away from her, and she no longer knew what was real and what wasn't. She walked into work slowly. Was the elevator always that exact color of brown? Maybe they'd changed the bulbs, and it just looked different. She walked out to see Barry standing there with the stopwatch.

"Barry, are you back doing that?" said Susan.

"Back doing it, Susan? I've been doing this every morning for longer than you've worked here."

"Oh," she said, distinctly remembering that he hadn't stood there for at least five years. Maybe she was just always early. "Well then, Barry, am I late? Do you want to fire me?"

"Oh Susan, we couldn't fire you. You are the backbone of this company." He nodded his head at her and she walked through to her office. It had a window. Only took five years to earn a room with a window, but she never looked at it. She was always looking down at her computer screen. Was she really the backbone of the company? Or just a cog that had been in place so long spinning that no one took any notice of it? The sign on her door said Financial Director, but she didn't direct anyone, and no one really asked anything of her. She did her reports. She kept the vendors paid. She could go all day without an actual conversation, just emails and text messages to the various other departments. She could do this job with her eyes closed. And maybe that was the problem. She'd just been going through her life with her eyes closed. The fountain had always been there, the elevator had always been that puked-up yellow-brown. Everything was fine. She was just imagining everything.

Lunch time came around and she pulled out the sandwich she'd brought from home. Every day, that was what she did. Eat the sandwich she brought, sit in her office all alone. She thought she should break the routine at least a bit. She walked into the lunchroom. Beverly and Giles were there. They worked in Sales.

"Mandala effect, Beverly. You should look at these." He leaned closer and put his phone up to her face. "Jif peanut butter, Beverly, not Jiffy."

"That can't be right. And are they kidding about the monopoly guy?"

"What's the mandala effect?" Susan asked, loading a plastic pod into the Keurig machine for a coffee.

"Oh, nothing," said Giles.

"But it's weird, right?" said Beverly. "Well, not you, Susan, but well..."

Susan took her coffee out from under the machine. "Ok, I'll see you guys later." They could just go back to doing what they were doing. They didn't want her around while they were flirting. Her chances to flirt at the office were all gone. Twenty years ago, when she'd started with the company, she'd flirted a little with a guy in Legal, Dan. She'd been too young then to realize he wasn't into women. And now, twenty years later, she was too old to flirt with any of the twenty- and thirty-somethings that came and went from the sales office and the rest of the executive team she knew too well. They were either married or unmarriageable, and she'd realized somewhere in those years that maybe she was unmarriageable too.

She took the coffee and went back to her desk, but the restlessness was unrelenting. So she went back to the elevator and back down to the first floor and took herself out walking on Sunset Boulevard. It had changed over the years. She was still in the old Wells Fargo bank building on the second floor, but the building across the street was new, all expensive condos and retail below. And the building on the other corner across from the statue was new, too. She remembers it arising like a black glass block in the sky. She needed a walk.

Walking down the street, the air smelled like Los Angeles; burned and used, while the faint trace of urine was detectible coming from the sidewalk. A homeless man was curled up in front of the famous Cinerama Dome, which had closed down during the pandemic and not reopened. The man opened up his eyes and yelled at her as she passed. "We are all sliding. You, lady, you are sliding."

She turned to him, and his eyes bored into her. "You've felt it. You know you have. Think! Think! Does all this look right to you, lady?"

She walked past quickly, driven by his smell, his words, and her own fear. A lingering fear—not of him, but of this sense that something was wrong. She was hungry. Some food would help. Her knee was hurting. No point in walking further. She turned and walked back in front of the Cinerama Dome. The man was gone, and she breathed out, not realizing she had been holding her breath. She bought some Veggie Grill for lunch. Fake meat seemed like it should be healthy at least. She'd keep the lunch she'd brought with her and eat it later before she went home.

She peeked over at the statue in front of the Chase Bank and shook her head.

Back in the office, she found herself googling again. The building wasn't the original one there. From 1938 to 1964 it had been the NBC Radio City. The building had been beautiful, a "moderne" building meant to last forever, and it had been razed to the ground less than 30 years later. When had the statue been put there, she wondered again.

The original was made in 1925 and it was a tiny little thing. How had it blown up and landed on the sidewalk near her office? She rubbed her sore knee and turned to look down through the slats in her blind. The sky was clear today. She remembered in the 1990s on a bad day, with bad smog, she couldn't see the street for the brown haze. She turned the wand and closed the slats, blocking out the last of the day, and went back to the accounts, shoveling in her food without thinking while she accepted transactions into the bank account.

Mandala effect—the term had fixed in her brain. What was that all about? She'd have to google it, maybe later, after she reconciled the account.

Saturday morning, she woke up early, realized she had no work to go to and forced herself to roll back over into the middle of her queen size bed and go back to sleep. She woke again and looked around the room; she needed to dust the bookshelf. Better to go out for breakfast than make a mess in the clean kitchen.

She pulled out her computer. What was that thing that she was going to google? Man-something; she'd remember later.

She went out to her silver Prius, and it looked wrong. There was white paint and a dent on the right rear corner. She hadn't done it, so one of her neighbors must have hit her overnight. She groaned. The car was paid off, and she'd dropped down to just liability insurance. She didn't have enough insurance to get the car repaired. The joy of being loyal to one company for so long was that she hadn't gotten the salary she would have gotten if she had moved to a new job. She kept thinking about moving, or asking for what she was worth, but she was comfortable, and change was hard. She hated change.

Pulling the Prius out, she looked for a white vehicle with the marks she knew would have been made by her car. She wanted them to pay for the repair. She wanted not to have to deal with the repair in the first place. Angry, she decided to drive to clear her head. Even with a Prius she took public transport. It saved a little money, and it was good for the planet, and she didn't have to spend the hour or so in stop-and-go traffic. She'd had the car six years, and it was paid off. How dare someone else ruin it? She found herself headed towards the airport and thought she would go to the In-N-Out by the runway and watch some planes land. It was something she used to do with her brother. He'd tell her what model the plane was and what its maximum speed and wingspan were, and she would just try to imagine where the plane had come from, and what the people onboard were coming to Los Angeles for.

She made the left off the freeway along Sepulveda and under the runway. She remembered the first time she'd landed at LAX all those years ago on the way home from a trip to Grandma; she thought the cars were going to hit the plane, then they all dove down into a tunnel and the plane landed above them. She entered the tunnel, and it was moving slowly. Too many people leaving, or coming, or something. She hadn't been on a plane for twenty-five years, not since she'd flown to Grandma's funeral. Looking left, she saw them. The doors. Doors in the middle of the tunnel.

Doors with glass windows with light shining through, doors in the concrete between the North-bound and South-bound side of the tunnel. And she knew with certainty that she had never seen those doors before. Not in all the times she had passed through this tunnel. Not in all the times she'd picked friends and family up from the airport, not in all the times she'd come to the In-N-Out just to watch the big metal birds land.

She got out of the tunnel confused and instead of driving to In-N-Out and getting an animal-style burger, she found a place to safely make a turn and went back through the tunnel. The other side of the tunnel divider had doors, too. In this reality, there were doors on both sides of what should have been a thin concrete divider between the lanes. And there was light between, like there were entire secret rooms in between the two sides of the tunnel. She had thought for sure when she'd seen the doors the first time that when she passed by them on the other side, she would see the back of the same doors. There were doors on this side, but they weren't matching doors. They were completely different doors. She couldn't have been more surprised if she'd walked in on Area 51 during an alien autopsy. These doors shouldn't exist. There was no way she'd driven through this tunnel so many times without seeing them. She was obviously going insane. What other possibilities were there?

She drove home, didn't hit traffic, yet somehow it took an extra half hour. She stumbled into the house feeling her sore knee, feeling exhausted, knowing she needed to sleep, knowing she needed to take ibuprofen and ice her sore leg, but instead she fell on her computer. She googled "doors in the airport LAX tunnel" and only found one Reddit from ten years before, someone asking why there were so many creepy-looking doors. No answers.

She got up and took the ibuprofen and went to bed. When she woke in the morning, all her worry was gone. Of course there were doors in the tunnel. She'd always been in a hurry and just not seen them. And that statue. She could almost remember seeing the statute... almost but not quite. Still, it was obviously there. She walked out to her car and looked at it. The dent she thought she'd seen yesterday was gone. She walked around to the other side to see if it was there. Nothing. She must have imagined it. Maybe it was just some dust or something. But she knew it wasn't, and she ran her hands over both sides of the car looking for the white paint and scrape she'd seen on it yesterday.

She got to work late. Barry wasn't standing there. She ran into him in the coffee room trying to make the Keurig machine spit out a coffee. "Hey, Barry. Not out by the elevator today?"

"Why would I do that, Susan? I haven't done that in years."

Of course he hadn't stood out there with a stopwatch for years. What was she thinking? She grabbed a paper cup and got in line to make herself some morning caffeine.

Beverly walked in, talking to Tania. "Yeah, Mandala effect. Franklin was telling me about it last week. You know, where a bunch of people remember something but it turns out it never happened. Like apparently Darth Vader never said, "Luke, I am your father.""

Tania stopped, confused. "Then what did he say?"

Beverly had her phone open, and she handed it to Tania. "See, like, did you think the monopoly guy had a monocle?"

Beverly threw her lunch in the fridge and turned to grab her phone and go out. "Do you mind if I look at that?" asked Susan.

"Sure, no problem," said Beverly, and Tania handed the phone over.

Mandala effect—that was what she had been meaning to look up. Jiff peanut butter, Sketchers shoes... was nothing the way she thought it should be? She handed back the phone and went to sit at her desk. She pulled up more Mandala effects.

Someone said it was just people remembering wrong. Someone else said it was proof of parallel universes, different realities. Somehow, this made more sense. It made more sense to her that Nelson Mandela had died in prison in a different reality than that millions of people just randomly decided to think he was dead for no reason. Maybe they were right, maybe there were parallel universes. She didn't want to open the shades and look to see if the statue was there. Maybe she was just slip-sliding through different realities. Maybe everyone was. She stretched out her leg and her knee didn't hurt. She didn't know when it had stopped. She shut down the website of Mandala effects, opened up her QuickBooks and went back to work.

Her memories would regroup and it would all be normal soon. She was a sensible woman and she really didn't like change.

Chapter 10

Alone Again, Naturally

The Natural Order—a political, racial, economic, religious catch-phrase. Take it deeper into Zoology, Biology, Geology and it's a map, to place things where we can find them. Astronomy and Cosmology too.

But what about a deeper question? Are you alive? And what happens when the maps and catchphrases don't answer? Whom do you ask then?

Janet died 5 years, 7 months, 11 days ago. It's easy to keep track. She died on the first. First of May, May Day. She used to love things like May Day. She'd tell the children about May Day festivals and when they were young, she made them a pole with ribbons to dance around. By the time Maxine was 8, she told her mother it was silly, and after that, Janet saved her holiday cheer for the more usual holidays, like Easter, Christmas or Thanksgiving. Thanksgiving was her chance to show everyone how much she loved them, with a table of never fewer than 20 people, friends and family, and so much food. She always decorated the whole house, not just the tree. The bathroom would have little Christmas-themed mats around the toilet, and Christmas hand towels. One year, we even had Christmas toilet paper. I didn't ask why; it was pretty odd to wipe my ass with a picture of a pine tree, but if it made her happy, who was I to complain?

She was a good wife in a way that isn't appreciated so much anymore. She kept the house clean. She was always such a good cook. I never in my married life had to worry that I'd come home and there wouldn't be something to eat. If she was too busy to fix dinner with something or another, there were always leftovers in the fridge—a pot roast—and desert—a pie or something. She was so well prepared. I never even thought about it. There was always enough of everything. We both had jobs and yet, somehow, she was always there for the kids when they needed her and there for me, too.

My God, I miss her. There isn't a day that goes by that I don't think about her, that I don't wonder why I am still here when she is gone. We met in college—Brigham Young. Neither of us were Mormons, but we'd gone there. To meet each other, she said, and maybe she was right. It was a good life. Until the last year or so it was a good life. You don't always appreciate that life is good in the moments that it is. You don't always appreciate when everything is going well. You don't think about it. You just go through the moments one day at a time and the only days that stand out looking back are the bad ones. And there were so few bad ones. So few that I can genuinely recall in vivid detail, so few days that I remember well at all. All the days were good—not great perhaps, not exciting, but that was hardly her fault.

There weren't a lot of vacations—the budget never allowed—but we had each other, and the kids. And the kids all grew up to be decent people. Even Maxine, who was such a handful as a teenager, finally found her place in the world. She's a schoolteacher now, screaming at other people's children instead of her mother. Michael and Morgan are doing well too. He's an engineer like his old man, except while I worked for the city in the urban planning department he's been off working on big projects. He was in Dubai last year; some kind of project that involved engineering an artificial island and water recycling facility. They think very highly of him and he's very successful, at least at work. His mother used to worry because he doesn't have a wife, or anyone who really loves him. "He's too old to still be alone," Janet would say.

Morgan is the one who is most like her mom. With a soft, gentle smile and her mother's eyes. When I see her smile, it reminds me of when Janet was young, and I want to smile with her, and also cry because it's not fair. Morgan married a decent guy, and she doesn't have to work. She's home with the three boys. "Three boys," Janet would always say. "I wish she'd had a girl. Boys are exhausting, but girls know how to wound their mother's soul." I knew what she meant by that. As much as Janet loved our kids, she never had problems with Michael. The girls were the ones that tried her, that tested her. They were the ones that spoke back and blamed all their problems on her. They lied, they stole money from her purse when they were teenagers, and they both did everything possible in different ways to make Janet crazy. Maxine and she would have screaming fights. Morgan was the one who would agree to do everything her mother asked and then just do nothing. I would catch the dishes later in the night and load the dishwasher myself rather than hear the fight between mom and daughter.

She loved them so much. All of them. She wanted what was best for them. They were all in good places in their lives when she got sick, and I think that helped her. Dying when they were teenagers would have seemed like a betrayal to her. For myself, I think leaving me alone was a betrayal. She was never supposed to die first.

We'd have those discussions... you know, the kind one has where you plan for the future. "When you die, love, I have been thinking I will just move in with my sister Bev."

"Really? Why?"

"Because I've always lived with someone—my family, then you—and I don't really want to live alone. You wouldn't want me living alone, would you?"

And I'd answered that I wouldn't, because after all, who would want to live alone? And here I was, after all that planning, after all those discussions when she'd still been healthy, living without her. Living alone. Five years of living alone because I didn't want to be a burden on our children, and I wasn't really sure any of them really wanted me. I've begun to worry about what might happen if I live long enough to become completely senile, because I don't really think I could ever live with any of them. Not Michael; he's too unstable, always rushing off somewhere for the next job. He can't even keep a relationship or a houseplant alive. Not Maxine, because honestly, she's just mean and impatient and I don't think that will work well at all. And not Morgan, because bless her heart, Morgan's got her hands full just with the three boys and the husband. So, I guess if I live too long I'll be in a home.

My friend Felix suggested to me that I find a girlfriend, someone who cooks well, can clean well enough, and just move on. But how does one move on? How do you forget the one person who got you that far in life and just move on to someone else? I know it would solve a lot of very practical problems but I am not ready to replace Janet, and I don't know if I ever will be.

Felix came over last week and opened the hall closet to hang up his coat... actually, I think it was really because he's a big busybody. Anyway, he opened the hall closet and Janet's winter coat was still there. And her umbrella and rainboots.

"Oh my God, Max," he said, turning from the closet to face me standing against the wallpaper wall, the blue trailing flower pattern Janet had bought and hung. "Don't tell me you haven't thrown her clothes out yet."

"Well," I said, not wanting to tell him the truth. The truth that I hadn't thrown out anything. The book she had been reading was still on the bedside table on her side of the bed. Her nightdress was still hanging in the bathroom, the chest of drawers was still packed with her clothes. Her perfume was still sitting on her dresser. The girls keep telling me that they will come over and sort out Mom's things and help me get rid of them, but I don't want to get rid of them. I don't want to get rid of all the things that remind me of my wife.

So I tell them no, and I hire a cleaning lady who once a week comes and makes sure that the dust is gone from around her things. And then the things are laid back down in the places they will never leave. The copy of Ken Follet's *Pillars of the Earth* she had by the bed wouldn't shut now even if I wanted to shut it. It's been open at that page for more than five years, holding the new shape until that is its shape. That is much like my life. I was torn open and rearranged into a new shape, and it's been five years but I am now twisted into this new shape and I don't know any other way to be.

The only thing that actually changed is Billy the cat. Janet didn't like cats, said she was allergic, and maybe she was a bit. You know, a bit of sneezing and needing a Claritin if we visited her friends that had cats, but not anything too much. I have always liked cats. When I was a kid, a stray cat brought her kittens into our house on a cold night and left them in my sock drawer. We kept the kittens as pets, at least the two that survived, but we never did manage to catch the mother. My mom wanted to go take her to get her fixed so she wouldn't keep bringing us her kittens to raise but she never brought us any extra kittens, just Black and White, named for their colors by a six-year-old who loved them. White died the year before I met Janet, and Janet told me if he hadn't, we would never have gotten together. She didn't date men who made her sneeze, which seemed fair enough.

Two Christmases ago Morgan decided I needed something to cuddle at night and showed up with Billy. He was a tiny little thing that had been found in a dumpster. It was love at first sight. And I found comfort in his tiny ticking noise, sleeping quietly against my chest.

I suppose you could say I've adjusted, become well-adjusted, whatever that means, proving that one can adjust to being alone even after years of being half of a whole. It means, I guess, that a wounded soul torn away from the one they thought was their other half can still limp through life, so long as they have a little cat snuggling them at night.

When I went to bed that night, it was a normal night. I'd done the dishes. I don't cook much; it wasn't something I ever did while Janet was here, but I got one of those meal boxes—Maxine set it up for me after Janet died—and well, groceries show up with clear directions, so I cook dinner. And before I go to bed I do all the dishes, by hand because the dishwasher died after Janet did. I didn't know you needed to run it and I just left it for a couple of months. Didn't seem any point to run it for one or two plates, and back then I was eating most of my meals out of the plastic microwave trays they'd come out of the freezer in. Anyway, it was a normal night, me doing the dishes while Billy rubbed himself against my feet. And then I fell into bed with a book. Didn't finish much before I turned off the light and rolled over.

I woke up early to pee. It's one of those things no one ever told you growing up—that one day you'd be awake at dawn trying to get the last few drops to fall through the broken plumbing. I noticed Billy's absence as I rose, that lack of warmth, but I figured he had his own plumbing to take care of in the dawn hours. I got back into the bed, rolled over, and hit something. I opened my eyes.

There was someone in the bed. I stifled a scream and turned on the light.

"Turn the light off, love," moaned Janet, and rolled back over.

"What are you doing here?"

"Be quiet. I'm trying to sleep."

It sounded like Janet. I poked her shoulder. She felt real. I got out of the bed and walked around. She looked real. This wasn't possible.

Had I wished she were alive? Oh, so many times. Had I wanted her back? More than words would say. And here she was. It must be a dream. I must be dreaming. This wasn't possible. I walked out to the sofa and lay down on it. I hoped Billy would join me. And somehow, as the sun rose, I slept, or at least in my dreaming state felt like I slept.

"What are you doing on the sofa, darling?"

I sat up and screamed. There stood Janet in the green dress with the yellow zigzag pattern I hadn't had the will to throw out.

"Oh, sorry to startle you. You must have had a bad night's sleep. Go back to bed. I'll make some coffee and you can have some later."

I stared. She looked real. It was daylight. The sun was shining. I watched her walk towards the kitchen in her sensible white shoes and green dress and I pinched myself, but she was still there. I grabbed my new iPhone from the stand by the bed and called Maxine.

"Hi, Dad. What's up? Are you and Mom coming around later, like you planned?"

"Me and Mom?"

"Yeah, remember we were talking about doing a BBQ today? I have all this fresh corn."

"What's the date?"

"Oh Dad, are you starting to lose it? It's Saturday, November 11, 2023."

I thought, yep, that's right, it's Veterans Day. I was going to spend it with Maxine, and Morgan was talking about coming over.

"Oh yeah, Veterans Day."

"Exactly, and since Mom is doing Thanksgiving next week at your house, we thought you guys should come here for Veterans Day. The weather is still warm enough for the grill, so Tom's going to fire it up. Morgan will be over later with her boys. We're going to see if the new game system can keep them quiet."

"Has it always been in the plans that Mom does Thanksgiving?" I asked, not sure how to broach the subject and ask whether or not Mom had been dead up until yesterday.

"Of course she always does Thanksgiving. It's her thing. Remember last year she finally let us come help set the table and bring drinks, but the big Thanksgiving turkey thing—that's her thing, not ours."

"Yeah..." I said, feeling confused, the whole world spinning around inside my head.

"Have you ever been tested for the BRCA mutation?"

"The what, Dad? Look, I'll see you later. We can talk then."

She should know what the BRCA mutation was. It was the genetic mutation that had allowed the cancer to kill her mother. Morgan had been tested for it and didn't have it, she would die some other way, and they'd been talking for the better part of a year whether Maxine was going to get tested. Now Maxine didn't know what I was talking about and Janet wasn't dead.

Maybe I was just asleep. Or hallucinating. Or I had died and gone to heaven, a heaven where Janet didn't die. I didn't know what to think. I was also exhausted. Maybe if I went back to sleep I would wake up and everything would make sense again. I called Billy but he didn't come.

"What are you doing, babe?" Janet said walking in with a cup of coffee. It smelled heavenly. Somehow making coffee for myself it never smelled so good.

"Calling Billy."

"Who's Billy?" she said, looking at my phone.

"Billy the cat."

"You are funnier and funnier the longer we are married. You know I'm allergic to cats. If there were one in the house I'd be sneezing. There isn't any cat here."

I forced myself not to drink the coffee. I just knew I had to go back to sleep. I had to get back to my life. I had to wake up snuggling a purring little ball of fur and knowing the shape of my day and my life.

It took some time but finally I fell back asleep into a strange dream where Janet had never died and it was almost Thanksgiving, and I didn't have a cat. I wondered, as one does when they are sleeping, what would have happened to Billy if he hadn't become my cat and then, somehow, I was dreaming about him and he was a tough alley cat, kind of like the one in the *Aristocats* movie I'd watched on video with the kids when they were little. It had good music, I remembered, and now I was on the dance floor with Janet, dancing to a big band playing swing music, yet I am pretty sure I have never learned to swing-dance, but it was a dream and I was so happy to have her in my arms again. And then I heard a ringing, and I woke up and reached for the phone.

"Hi, Dad. Mom isn't picking up her phone. Can you ask her if she has any of those corn-on-the-cob holder things? It will make it so much easier to eat the corn I bought."

"Corn? Mom?" I was still half asleep.

"Yes, Dad. Can you just call Mom to come to the phone? I'll ask her directly."

"Mom? Oh. Janet." I called, "Janet." I don't know what I really expected, but Janet walked in and I passed my phone up to her.

"Yes, of course I have corn-on-the-cob holders. Sure, I can bring them. I actually have two sets if you want to keep one." I was staring up. She looked like Janet. I pinched myself hard.

"Oww."

"What's the problem, Dad?" I had forgotten she called me Dad, especially when she'd just been talking to our daughters. Now that I heard it, I wasn't sure I liked it.

"Nothing." Everything. Oh my God, it wasn't a dream. What the hell was going on? What could I say? Janet, you should be dead? Why aren't you dead? Everyone else didn't think she was dead. The girls were calling the way they always did when she was alive for every little thing, talking to her instead of me. I can't say anything. They will think I am insane. I am just lucky. I've been given what I wanted most in the world—more time with the love of my life. Yes, I told myself, breathing in, there is no problem. I am so lucky.

Janet was in her element with her grandkids buzzing about while Tom got the grill going. It was still warm, too warm for November, really. Just another thing that was wrong with the world, I thought. I sat by the pool. Janet was the focus, and I was her chauffeur. I realized it had always been that way. It wasn't till after she was gone that the girls had started calling to talk to me. It wasn't until my lovely wife was dead that my grandkids started to run up and hug me. With Janet there, they always ran to her first to see what gift or candy she'd brought for them. She got the hugs and the attention and I got a "Hi, Granddad," as they ran off with the new water pistols Grandma had just happened to pick up for them.

Some things never changed. Janet's purse was still a mystery to me. Somehow it contained everything you could ever want, from a roll of antacids to a water pistol, candy to car insurance papers, and yet somehow she managed to carry it without the weight pulling her over.

I walked over to the pool. The smoke from the barbeque had forced me out of my deck chair. The water looked nice. I bent over and put in a finger and it was freezing like I knew it would be. It felt real, cold, wet and real. Everything felt real. Janet looked real. But the five years, almost six years, felt real too. I was obviously going insane.

"Tom," I said, walking back away from the pool. "How can you tell if you've had a stroke?"

I figured he should know. He'd only been an EMT for 15 years.

"Are you alright?" Tom said, turning around. "What's going on?"

"Oh nothing. I'm fine, just a friend of mine had a mini stroke and—"

"Well, so long as you're feeling ok," Tom said, turning back to the hot dogs on the grill. "You should really get to a hospital as soon as possible if you think you've had a stroke, otherwise the damage could be permanent."

"What kind of damage?"

"Paralysis, blurred vision, problems speaking, you know, brain damage symptoms." He was taking all the food off the grill, so it would be time to go inside soon with the three most important women of my life. Three women whom, right now, I didn't feel strong enough to talk to. What should I say around the dinner table? Maxine, go get your boobs checked; they will need to take out a lump? Or, Morgan, in my world you are already talking about a double mastectomy after they found that BRCA variant. Or how about, Janet, my love, how does it feel to be alive, because as far as I remember, you've been dead for a while now? I didn't have any of the symptoms Tom was talking about, so what on earth was wrong with me? What on earth was wrong with the universe?

On the ride home with Janet, I said, "Honey, what would you do if I died and came back?"

"Oh, honey, you say the strangest things. What do you mean? Like you had a heart attack and they brought you back?"

I took my eyes off the road and turned to her; she was looking at her phone, not looking at me at all. "No, like I was dead for a while and then I was alive."

"Wow, yeah, I don't believe in zombies. Last recorded resurrection was Christ, and that was a while ago. "I didn't turn to look at her, but kept driving. "What if people resurrected all the time and just no one talked about it because..."

"Don't be silly, love. If the dead came back, that would destroy the natural order. The dead need to stay dead. "This actually was the only thing she'd said since she came back that made sense to me. Somehow there was something off with the natural order. I looked over at her again, her hair draping across her face, working on a list of what to buy for Thanksgiving on her phone. I loved her. I still loved her. I would always love her. But what were the consequences of the natural order being upset? I started thinking that I may need to restore order to the universe. And my heart ached.

Chapter 11

Hospital Dreams

A modern, functioning hospital is the saddest clean, well-lighted place on Earth. People go there to get well, and often die in the process. Overworked nurses and doctors break down, or kill themselves. To deal with this overwhelming weight some people fall back on rationalization and the only medicine left to them: hope.

It's night three on the sofa in the hospital room. They let me stay because even though she's an adult, they understand that a mom wants to be with her child at a time like this. And they understood that the child also needed her mother.

I am in the same dress we came to the emergency room in. It seems like a hundred years ago. I had to drag her there. "Mom, you worry too much. I'm fine, just a little tired."

She was pale yellow with gray circles around her eyes. She didn't look twenty. She looked 60. "There is something wrong. You shouldn't be struggling to get up the stairs."

It had been weeks since she looked well, but always, "I'm fine, Mom, just tired." It was time. Even if they just told us there was nothing wrong with her, I needed to know.

I have always avoided doctors and hospitals. I have probably passed this down to my children. And in general, I still think it's a good idea. Not rushing to doctors until they were needed. I just felt like it was needed. I wondered if I'd been a different kind of mother if I'd taken her to more doctors as a kid, whether she would have taken herself to the doctor earlier. I thought we'd be in the waiting room for a couple of hours, see a doctor, then go home. Instead, they took her blood pressure and pulse, put her in a wheelchair and rolled us in.

I should have panicked then. In the next room, she climbed into a hospital gown and hospital bed. Looking so small, hooked up to all the machines that told the story. Her heart was running at 160 beats per minute and her blood pressure was so high.

The emergency room doctor spent time with her. I should have known that was wrong. And then another doctor came in. And in between they poked and prodded and took out blood and then more blood and ran more tests.

I was freezing, and I tried to keep her warm. Her little toes were so white and cold. Next time we come to the emergency room, I told myself, we will dress warm and bring woolen socks. Although I was hoping there would never be a next time. This was the first time I had ever been to an emergency room in my life and I was forty-eight years old. Forty-eight years of never really visiting doctors, never breaking a bone, or wounding myself enough to need stitches. Ok, in reality, the scar on my hand probably wouldn't be there if my mom had taken me to a doctor and gotten stitches, but my mom didn't believe in doctors. Doctors killed your grandmother, she told me repeatedly growing up. Don't go to hospital. Hospitals kill people. I'd been born at home and

Karin had been born in a birthing center. I hadn't wanted a hospital birth, but I also didn't want to clean my house before a doctor came over, so that was a compromise. Tommy sort of agreed, at least not enough to complain or argue, so that was agreement enough. In the end, it wasn't like he was planning to be there for me or Karin, and he wasn't. But one thing and another, this was my first time in an emergency room, and I didn't know what to expect.

"Karin, we want to put in another IV and start you on a blood transfusion," said the doctor, a new doctor, older and obviously senior to the first doctor.

Karin shuddered. She hated needles. This was all more than she'd signed up for. She looked at me, her eyes yellow and full of fear.

"Why?" I asked the doctor.

He explained to us carefully what was going on. The level of blood in her body was very low and her heart was running hard just to keep the blood she had circulating. Her organs were shutting down, which was why she was turning yellow. Her liver wasn't working properly. And he didn't know why she was so anemic. There just wasn't enough blood left to run her body. Then he told us she wasn't at the limit where it was necessary for the blood transfusion yet, but they wanted to be ready.

"Can we think about it?" I asked, seeing the terror on my baby's face.

"Yes," he said. "I'll run some more tests, verify your blood type. You have an hour to decide."

Later, the doctor would say it was an autoimmune condition. Later, we would learn that a blood transfusion was a dangerous option because her body could fight the new blood and trigger an even greater autoimmune response. For now, we didn't know this. We just had a bad feeling. But when the doctor came back and insisted, we told him to do the blood transfusion. The bad feeling grew. The nurse kept testing Karin's blood. The blood had been ordered from the blood bank and it was on its way.

The nurse was with us now. One of those women to whom sainthood should be conferred but who, after a long night of calm care, probably went home to unappreciative children and a husband who wanted her to make him something to eat. The nurse had the second IV in now, a thin plastic line coming from my pale thin girl. How had we gotten here?

How had that tiny little baby, then sweet, independent little girl, then defiant, angry teen turn into this frail, weak young lady? How had my darling girl gone from moving out and moving on with her life so proud and so independent to lying on a hospital bed with all of her organs failing?

The nurse made a sound. It sounded quietly victorious. "The latest test, your hematocrit, is over the borderline, Karin."

"What does that mean?" I said.

"I did it twice. I don't think the machine is reading her blood well because it's breaking down so fast. So I got the other machine. And her hematocrit—the red blood cells in your blood, Karin—they are higher than we thought. You don't have to have the transfusion if you don't want."

I knew what Karin was going to say. We'd both been afraid of the blood transfusion for reasons we couldn't even explain. I'd always told Karin to go with her gut feeling, and I knew her gut and mine were both scared about the blood transfusion. "No transfusion, thanks," said Karin.

"So glad I did that test again. I'll go tell them to stop warming the blood." The nurse walked out, and we stared at each other, somehow knowing we had just dodged a bullet but not knowing what other weapons were aimed at us.

Though I walk through the valley of the shadow of death, I shall fear no evil, for the nurses are on my side, a voice said in my head.

The cold of the room seemed to have seeped into my heart. I was numb now. And they told us she would be admitted, and we would be staying, and yet I was surprised. When I read the report the next day where the Emergency Room doctor had written that she was in imminent danger of multiorgan failure, it hit me then. They didn't send us home because they thought she was going to die. I hadn't even thought that was a possibility when we went to the hospital. But a trained professional had looked at my baby, looked at her vitals, and decided to keep her in hospital because she could die. Imminent organ failure. Imminent death.

This was the next day in the hospital after the first night on the sofa in the corner. I was still thinking we would go home soon. They were running enough tests on her to find out what it was soon. And then we'd leave.

By day two, it was obvious that the tests weren't telling anyone anything they wanted to share with us, or maybe that they even understood. My kid was sick, really sick, and they knew more about what it wasn't than what it was. Somehow, having a name for it would help. Not fix it. The name, they decided, was autoimmune hemolytic anemia. And they started to discuss treatment plans. I wanted to go home and wash, but I couldn't leave her alone in this place. She wanted to go home and sleep in a bed where no one woke her every four hours to poke her again. Her arms looked like someone had stabbed and run, with big blue bruises at her wrists and forearm. They'd had to reset one of the IVs and the other had a thin line of blood that had dripped out of it. Maybe it would need to be redone too. She looked so small and pale, and a fear gripped me. A fear that she would never leave the hospital, that she would die there while they tried to find out how to treat her. That this was the beginning of the end. Twenty years old and I would lose her.

I realized I could have lost her that first day in the ER before we were admitted. I could have lost her when they gave her the blood transfusion. That would have been a mistake, and we'd been so close to making it, so close to giving her blood, which may have triggered a reaction that shut down her kidneys and liver completely. She was still yellow. I could see it now in her arms, between the shiny new bruises, and in her tired eyes.

By day three we'd met most of the staff at the hospital. And I was still too scared to go home and change my clothes. I'd unbutton my cleavage at night, release my bra and sleep the sleep of the dead, until the nurse came at twelve, three, six and nine a.m., at which point I would stop pretending I could keep my eyes closed and open them for the next round of vitals and blood work.

The third night was different. I went to sleep anxious but so tired I managed to sleep through the midnight and three a.m. tests on that hard sofa with its thin cotton blanket and the dirty clothes. Then at six a.m. I woke up from a dream. And I was no longer scared or nervous. I looked over at my baby there on the bed, being poked and prodded again by the nurse, and I suddenly knew she was going to be ok. At least now.I'd dreamed that my granddaughter, as yet a dream in my daughter's mind, would have a baby. And my daughter, my little woman lying up there on that hospital bed so bravely and so small would die at the age of 47, just before her granddaughter was born, of a heart attack. And looking over at the hospital bed, I was happy.

I had dreamed in vivid detail of the death of my daughter, and I was happy. Because the death was not going to be today, because she was going to live long enough to have and raise a daughter. And she would die knowing her granddaughter was coming. I knew with certainty it was true. That this time in the hospital would end, and that my baby girl would survive, and that she would have a daughter soon. A beautiful, willful daughter. And I would need to stay healthy and strong because my granddaughter and great-granddaughter would need me. A tear leaked out of my eye because it would be sad, but I knew what I had to do.

Chapter 12

Spring Cleaning

*S*o many of our memories are attached to things. And why not?
People disappear or die or betray you, pets are replaced, but that
paperweight on your desk, the Waterford crystal goblet, the vacation
photographs will live forever. Or as long as you let them.

The hardest things to throw out are the things connected to projects. Projects you never started, or started but didn't finish. So the
half-knitted sweater in that beautiful bluish mauve wool—you have
six balls of the wool and a sweater that even if finished wouldn't fit
the person it had been intended for, because when the six balls of
wool were purchased, the child was six and now she's 45. The wool
is beautiful, and I should pull apart the half of the sweater that's
finished and knit something else. But I don't. And even if I did knit her
something from the wool now, she wouldn't want it. The colors would
be wrong, or something. If I'd finished it when she was six, maybe she
would have loved it. It's too late to find out now.

The second hardest thing to throw out are the things you bought
to organize yourself. The house is full of junk, so you buy containers

for the junk, and a label maker and labels. And then somehow the new containers and the label maker just become one more thing on the pile of detritus that is your life. But how do I throw out that pile of plastic containers I have in the garage, that pile that has been waiting so long for me to organize my bedroom?

The next hardest thing to let go of is the things given to you by another. That ugly clock your mom gave you that goes *dong* every hour as if you live in a train station and the train will be involved in a collision if it's not running on time. It doesn't normally wake you up. You are used to the periodic *dong* but all your guests wake screaming. Or that hideous painting Grandma left you that you hung in the guest room. You know, the one she got on her world tour from some artist sitting on the side of the Seine. It's a great story, just not a great painting. How do you get rid of that ugly painting? It belonged to your grandma; it hung in her house for 40 years. It's hung in your house for 40 years, and there is the story of Grandma walking in Paris on her great overseas trip when she was young and beautiful, long before you were born, and someone gave her a painting.

I need to spring-clean. It's time. I can't live like this, with all these things. The problem is that every item has a memory attached to it. The painting with the memory of my grandmother makes me smile but I also cry. It's been so long since she died. She had a long and happy life and yet I feel the lack of her in my life, a hole no one else has ever filled. I look around and everything in my life is filled with things, and I am tired. I am tired of all the things. And all the things have memories attached to them. That rug on the sofa, that's the one Maggie bought me for Christmas last year. She took her family to Bali for Christmas, so we did Christmas Dec 6th. Of course, the rug was something she'd ordered custom-made, so it arrived Jan 4th. Still, it's the thought that counts. That's what I said. And Christmas on the 6th was lovely, and then I ate leftovers for a week. By the time Christmas came along I spent it alone. I'd been invited to the neighbors but I didn't want to bring them down.

I hate that rug.

There's nothing in this house that doesn't have a memory, good or bad, attached. I am just tired. Tired of all the things, tired of all the memories. Tired of all of it.

I have had enough. I started to throw things into a box. It didn't feel good throwing things out, so I wasn't throwing them out. I was giving them to a charity so they could make money, maybe help some homeless people. That way I could justify getting rid of the books Adrian had loved. It's been so hard living without him, yet with all his things in every corner, with all the memories of how we bought the house together, how we lived a good life... and then he left me alone. I am so tired. I don't want to do this anymore.

The phone rang, and I picked it up. "Hi, Mom. You'll never guess what happened. Marc got promoted again and we are going to be moving to New York. I mean Upstate New York, but it will be amazing. They are paying for our move and we'll be able to afford a new house and they are providing a company car."

"That's nice, Maggie... Upstate New York—won't that be cold?"

"Well, of course it will, Mom, but you didn't expect us to stay in California, did you? It's too hot here these days, anyway. I don't remember the last time I went outside in the summer... you know, deliberately left the AC. I mean, we are never going to be able to afford our own house here. And you knew he was hoping for a promotion? I mean, I've been talking about it for so long. The kids can start school there in the fall and we'll have a white Christmas. I mean, I love white Christmases. Whenever we go and see his family in Pennsylvania, it is always so fun, and of course it's going to be great having his family close by. The kids can finally visit their cousins more often, maybe spend the summers together. It's going to be great."

"That's nice, dear. I am doing some spring-cleaning."

"Oh, I saw this thing on TV, Swedish Death Cleaning. You know, you throw away stuff your relatives aren't going to want. And you know I don't want any of your junk. I have enough junk of my own. And now that we are moving, I am going to have to throw out so much stuff."

"Yes, dear. I am ready to get rid of—"

"I have another call from Marc on the other line. Bye, Mom."

"But..." And the phone was dead in my hand. I put it down. Grabbed up the next plastic bag. The handmade doily my aunt brought me from Poland. Poor Aunt Joy. No one should lose their daughter at 43. Your children should outlive you. She was never happy after that. The cancer was just a blessing to end her pain. I can see her now in the hospital bed, so thin, her arms assaulted by tubes and needle scars and bruises, her collarbones now somehow the largest part of her entire body, jutting outward from the pillow. And poor cousin May—some autoimmune thing. What was it? I'd never heard of it before she was hospitalized. The doctors said she would be fine. I remember Joy and May still both hopeful, playing cards in the hospital to pass the time. They were going to do chemo and she'd be fine. No one knew then she was allergic to the chemo. I picked up the doily and threw it in the bag. It was beautiful, but all I saw when I looked at it were all those memories flooding back. Sad memories. So sad. I'd lived with them for so long. It was time. I was tired. So tired.

I should move. Just move and leave everything behind. But I am so tired. Maybe I should move to Upstate New York, but I'm not sure Maggie would really appreciate it. The coasters Adrian bought for me at that little art gallery in New Mexico when we were there visiting my friend Beth. They were lovely, and he saw how much I wanted them. I remember it so well. "Well, I suppose you got to buy something," he said. "And these don't cost much." He had walked them up to the counter and handed over the credit card. When we got back from that trip he had worried so much about what we had spent, he did so much overtime. That was the last time I visited Beth. She came out here once to visit, but it was difficult and now we just write cards once a year and call occasionally. When her husband dies, she says we should move in together, but he looks like he's going to go on forever. Not like my Adrian.

The first heart attack was a scare. I remember it so well. I was sitting in the car picking up Maggie from school when the phone rang. He'd been rushed to the ER from work. I sent Maggie home with a friend and found him in the ER in the hallway attached to an EKG, all the beeping and green lines wavering up and down, only telling me he was still alive. I'd cried all the way to the hospital. I had been so scared. He was only 52. He wasn't fat or out of shape. He didn't eat badly. When we went out he'd order a grilled chicken breast and a salad and I'd have a cheeseburger and french fries, just to piss him off. "You know, Margaret, you keep saying you want to lose weight, and then you order something like that?" And I'd order a chocolate shake and apple pie a la mode just because I could. And he wouldn't say anything by then. It wasn't like we ate out often; we were always saving. Most of my salary went into our retirement fund. He paid the rest of the bills. Because when we retired we wanted to travel. Except he never retired. They put the stents in, and the second heart attack two weeks after he got out of the hospital, when he was feeling fine, that was the one that killed him. Killed him dead in front of me, in our home. This home. This home filled with memories of him. The house we made together. I want to move. I want to forget. I am so tired. I put the coasters in the box to go.

I called the Salvation Army to come pick up the boxes. There were going to be too many for me to carry. That Marie Kondo woman tells you to keep the things that spark joy, but if I did that I'd be running around naked outside on the streets. I envy homeless people. If all I had was a shopping cart, then maybe I'd have it filled only with the things I need, but then maybe even the plastic tarp would hold memories of that time someone tried to knife me to get it. It's hard to know what is going on in another person's head.

Here on the shelf, a stone apple. A fundamentally useless thing, and there it sits, collecting dust with the china my other grandma gave me. The antique china that Maggie has never wanted. I have no one else to give it to. It's been in the family for four generations. And yes, some of it is broken and chipped and cracked, and there are those pieces I want to fix but I never have. Reminds me of my mother's ring, the one on my right hand. She was going to give it to me for my 21st birthday. It was beautiful—a ruby, a sapphire, an emerald, a sapphire and another ruby. I always liked it. So much prettier than the engagement ring my father gave her.

And then one of the stones fell out, and she replaced it with plastic, and another, and another, and she said she would give it to me when she got the stones replaced properly, only she never did. There was never money for that. Money for my father's next money-making scheme, money for twelve thousand greeting cards that rotted in the basement, money for exercise equipment that was never used, money for his classic car he never drove, but never money for that. And then my mom gave me the ring on her deathbed. If she hadn't, I would have buried her with it, sent that mess of plastic and rubies down deep under the ground. But she gave it to me and told me to restore it with the money from the estate. But I didn't. Adrian didn't think it was a good investment. He put the money into Bitcoin instead, before the crash.

I pulled the ring off my finger; it was stuck, my finger had swollen around it, grown bigger, almost eating it. I went to the sink and grabbed the bottle of dish detergent and poured it on. Slowly, turning and turning, it came off. I didn't need to remember any of that. I was too tired. I looked down at my left hand, at the rings Adrian had given me—his grandmother's engagement ring (not my style, but it was from him), and the plain gold band. I squirted the soap onto the other hand and began to pull and tug until they too came off.

I looked at those tiny gold bands in the sink, and my hands with the scars cut into the flesh from where they had come. My fingers had atrophied beneath them, the same way my love had atrophied over the years of marriage. The love had carved a scar through my soul but by then it had marked me forever. But that first love, the real love, the smile when you think of another, that joy when like meets like and together they are more than they could have ever dreamed... that had gone. I dried the rings and put them in a zip-lock bag in the box with the coasters. Someone might enjoy them. It had been long enough. And that stone apple, the one they gave me when I retired as a teacher. Engraved with my name. More useless than a gold watch. No one would ever want that. I picked it up; it was heavy in my hand. Forty years of teaching and I had a paperweight and a blur of memories of students' faces. So important in the day, but now all their names are gone and their faces blur together, a montage of braces, acne and hope. I throw the apple in the charity box. And then I reach down and take it out. No one will ever want this. I didn't want this. I walk over to the trash can and throw it in. It's liberating and sad.

Back to the china cabinet. My grandmother knew I was a wanderer, always moving from one house to another. I felt like the china was her attempt to anchor me. Give me a bunch of fragile belongings that would never travel well. Every time I boxed them up, every time I moved, I broke at least one thing. Moving into this house with Adrian all those years ago, the pieces finally had a home, a stable home. And there they have sat, gathering dust for forty years. Not that I haven't taken them out sometimes and had a tea party of washing them and just put them back in.

Maggie should want these. Of all my possessions, they are the ones that mean the most to me. They are the ones with the most happy memories. The tea parties I had with Maggie and my mom, and then Maggie and her daughter. These are the last things I have of my paternal grandmother. The grandma who was never outrageous or pretty enough to be given a painting while walking by the Seine. The grandma who taught me how to bake cakes. She's been gone so long the pain has faded and all I have is wonderful recipes and memories of food. I don't want to throw out her china. I called Maggie again.

"Hi, honey."

"I'm busy, Mom. What's up?"

"I am wondering if you want the china... you know, your grandma's china?"

"You interrupted me for that? You know I don't need that junk. And I'm moving again. What will I do with it? I don't need more stuff collecting dust. Just give it away. Got to go. Marc's calling."

And she hung up as quickly as possible while I was still saying goodbye. I said goodbye to a dial tone.

So I went and purchased some boxes to pack china, and bubble wrap, and started the slow process of wrapping up the fragile cups. I'd forgotten this. Here in one of the cups was a note written in my grandmother's precise schoolteacher printing. "This is the cup your great-grandmother used to drink her tea." It wasn't much of a cup, very small and not as pretty as some of the others, no flowers or patterns, just a small painted picture of a tall ship coming onto shore. I sat crying at the idea of the china going to Goodwill only to be broken and unimportant. My poor great-grandmother drank her tea from this tiny little cup. Somehow, this fragile piece had survived long enough to come to me. It should go to Maggie's kids. If they didn't want it, then throw it away. Throw it all away. Because if it meant that little, then so did I.

I rang the lawyer. His secretary put me through, and I made the request simple enough. "Hi, Bob." It seemed odd to call him Robert or Mr. Ignalt. After all, he was 20 years younger than me. "I was hoping to change my will." I'd never had a will before Adrian died, and he'd died without one. After that, I'd met Bob. I remember that meeting. "Well, Mrs.—"

"Call me Margaret. Please." I'd dressed up to go to his office feeling like my regular jeans and a t-shirt weren't enough to make a will with, weren't enough to decide the future of my child should I die. After all, Maggie was only seventeen, not yet eighteen, and I wanted to make sure she got to college. That she got a good life and the career she wanted. And I did. I kept her in school, I worked two jobs to keep the house, and when she graduated, I gave her a trip to Europe to celebrate. That was where she would meet Marc and decide to go on to get her Master's degree. So I kept the two jobs, and she got her Master's, and the will was never needed, the life insurance policy never paid out while she was young, and everything went well. As well as it can when you are left alone and your only child loses the one parent they truly love. But Bob had held my hand through all of it. Fresh out of law school back then, he was thinner. His suits were more expensive now and hung looser on his shoulders and tighter on his belly. He'd helped me make the hard decisions. "If, God forbid, you were in a coma, Margaret, would you want them to keep you on life support or pull the plug?"

"Pull the plug." I answered easily, even knowing that for Adrian I couldn't have done it.

"What if you don't need life support? What if you are just in a vegetative state?"

"I don't understand."

"I'll give you an example, Margaret. My grandma, sweet woman, got dementia. Lewy Body dementia. She was physically still fine. I mean, she didn't need life support, but she just stopped eating. And then one day she just wasn't really there, she just lay staring at the ceiling and wasting away. She was in a vegetative state. Would you want to be fed if you were like that or would you want to have food and/or liquids withheld?"

"You mean starve to death?"

"Yes, or—let's not sugarcoat this—your family will watch you starve or die of thirst."

"Wow."

"We'll come back to that one, Margaret. You should think about it and think about how your family would feel about your decisions. You also need to think about whether you would like to be resuscitated or whether you would want a DNR order."

"So if I had a heart attack, my daughter could call 911 and they couldn't try to resuscitate? No, that's unacceptable." What if Adrian hadn't been resuscitated the first time, and I'd had to stand there and watch him die? Well, I did stand there and watch him die and NO. None of this was ok.

Bob had seen my emotional turmoil and reached his hand out to me. "Let's start with the easy stuff. Who would you like to leave your house to?"

Bob was going to have to help me again. "Bob, could you set up a storage unit where I can leave some physical items for my oldest granddaughter?"

"How big? Oh, a small closet will do. I want to leave her my china and skip my daughter. I want her to receive it all when she is 20 years old, whether I am alive or not."

"What's her name?"

"Rose Margaret Alderson."

I could hear the clicking. "Oh yes, she's listed in your will already. She's sixteen now."

"Sixteen already. I thought she was younger. Yes, her." I recognized something of my own restlessness in her. And perhaps it was just a mean joke, but I was going to do to her what my grandmother had done to me—give her fragile and precious things to try to keep intact throughout her life. It seemed only fair.

I got off the phone with Bob and everything was, as they say, "your uncle." He would have the movers around tomorrow to move and store the china and put it away for her.

I went to the photograph albums and threw them all in a box too. They would go to Rose as well, in that closet paid for by my estate until she was twenty. I had been twenty when my grandmother gave me all her things. I put the box by the door. All those dusty photos taken with a film camera. And older sepia prints, fading, of people I didn't always know the name of anymore. The tape closing the boxes felt final.

I went to my bedroom and opened Adrian's part of the closet. There it all was. All his things I could never throw out. His shirts still hanging ironed from the last time I had ironed them. His suit was still in the bag back from the cleaners. The suit I'd only picked up the day before he died. The shoes. Three pairs of leather dress shoes, each more uncomfortable than the last, but his one call to vanity, shined by his own hand and almost but not quite broken in. I opened the garbage bag, glad I'd gotten the very strong ones. This would be heavy for the Salvation Army pickup guys, but these dated dress-up clothes of days gone by had to go. I pulled out the drawers of cufflinks and belts and tipped them into the bag. It would have been nice if Maggie had helped me with this, but like she'd said, she was too busy moving house again.

I took the things off the wardrobe hangers and folded them into the bag, not wanting to empty the wardrobe, a space that had been filed for so long. There was nothing left of him now. I was so tired of holding on to him, holding on to the memories. That blue shirt, that's the one he thought made his eyes pop, and that tie pin. I'd bought that for him on our fifth anniversary. All these things, these useless things with all these memories. Everything a memory, every memory a sorrow.

By the time the Salvation Army came, the house was empty of things, empty of so many things. They gathered up the bags and boxes and took them away and I was left alone in my clean, spacious house filled with light and air and little else. I looked around the room, feeling free, feeling nothing.

The phone rang, and I picked it up. "Hello."

"Hi. Can you take the dog for the weekend? We are going to take Rose to look at NYU."

"What dog?"

"Max, Mom. Jesus."

"Mom? Who are you?" I looked around my beautiful empty house. Who was this woman? She must have dialed the wrong number. I didn't have a daughter.

"Mom, it's Maggie."

"Maggie? I don't know any Maggie," I said and put the phone back down. It started to ring again. I looked over at the phone. Maggie, it said. I didn't know any Maggie. Who was she? I didn't need to talk to anyone I didn't know.

I walked back to my bedroom and lay down on my clean bed in my empty room. The phone kept ringing out on the empty shelf.

Chapter 13

Ultimate Keto Diet

Hollywood has its own rules. Hell, its own reality. Everyone is loosely controlled by the star system, and tightly by their own egos. The limitations of their talents and their bodies make for nervous days and sleepless nights, and rare is the one who is not looking for the magic elixir that will turn back time to their highest peak performance. And occasionally the unlucky ones find it.

It's hard to stay in shape at my age. Hell, it's hard to stay in shape when you're younger, but the older I get, the more I have to work at it. My face is my job. No one wants to see me with a dad bod floating across the screen 40 feet tall with a beer gut. That's the truth. It's an ugly truth, but I don't get roles because I am a great actor, or because I'm fun to work with. I get roles because women come out to the movie and I get enough box office to get the next job. Ok, and maybe gay men too, but you know what I mean.

I am the guy who is still supposed to take his shirt off in at least one scene. And I go to the gym every day. It's not just luck that I still have a six-pack at 52. I work hard. I need people to understand this. Everyone is so quick to judge. You think, he's a celebrity. He could just stop working. But you are so wrong. I can't stop working. I can barely keep up paying the alimony on my last divorce. You watched that one with glee while it raced across your TV set, didn't you, and when they found the love child, I'm sure you ate that up too. So now I'm paying child support to twelve children. Most of them were youthful indiscretions. I mean, when you're young, you don't say no to anything that's offered to you. And I was young when I hit the big time. Too young to save anything. Hell, I didn't even buy a house, just lived at the Chateau Marmont when I was in LA and whatever the most expensive place was everywhere else. And the amount of money I snorted or shot up or dropped would make the chairman of the Fed blush. Back then I could do anything, stay up four days straight on a diet of mezcal and coke and still do the love scene on set. I was young and invincible, and I thought I always would be.

I think that's why 35 hit me so hard. Because for actors 35 is the new 50. If you hit 35, you either have to look like a 20-year-old or try to look like a 20-year-old. And my body just broke down. You should have seen the pictures in the tabloids. Well, you probably did see the pictures in the tabloids. *National Enquirer*, God bless them, said I was bulking up for a part, that I'd been cast in a serious role. Which was exactly the story my publicist was putting out. There's someone else I've bought a house for, and probably paid for college for her kids, but at least she's done something for the money, not like that broad I married in Vegas. What was her name again? Marie... I think it was Marie, or was it Maria? I should remember. That cost me a million dollars because I wasn't actually divorced from Priscilla and Priscilla wasn't ready to give up on me then. Later, yes, but not then.

It was the diet that finally drove Priscilla away. The cheating she was fine with, the hours in the gym, the coke, the vodka, but when I went clean and went Keto, that's when she left. Well, not exactly when I started the Keto. When I started that she was onboard. Bacon for breakfast, filet mignon for lunch, those little Atkins candy bars everywhere. I actually want to know what god Rob Lowe sacrifices to, because those things made me gain pooch in areas I didn't know it could grow.

How does a full-grown man all of a sudden get a second butt below his first one? I tried all the standard diets. God knows I did. I went vegan. I went Paleo. It was finally my trainer that suggested I go Carnivore. Nothing but meat. And salt and water. Not particularly exciting, I got to tell you. I think Pricilla was staying at that point for the trainer. Because God knows I was glad we had a 20,000 square foot house. At least I didn't have to run into her often.

National Enquirer said that we were in couples' counseling and trying to bring back our love. I vaguely remembered she'd suggested therapy, but I didn't remember her assistant or mine booking us in to go together. Just getting to therapy alone was hard enough.

And I'm not suggesting the baby isn't mine. I was pretty sure he was, even before the DNA test. Because occasionally when you're alone and you're lonely you think that you and your ex still have something. He was conceived sometime in between her leaving and her staying gone.

It was about that time I was up for the part as the action hero in that movie based on that series of books about a Mafia hitman who becomes a CIA agent; you know the one I'm talking about. You know, that kind of series can keep an actor busy for 20 years; I mean, if Tom

Cruise manages to stay upright and lucid, he'll be starring in *Mission Impossible* movies when he's 94. Anyway, it was a big chance for me. I was up against some heavy hitters; you know, every aging actor in Hollywood is trying to be an action hero these days. I'm not saying you are going to see me shirtless at 80, like Harrison Ford, but I got to take my shirt off to get pretty much any role. I mean, I kind of hope they will still be casting me when I'm 80, but it's unlikely. I'm not stupid. I know I'm not a great actor. I'm a decent actor. I am easy to work with; I know my lines, but I'm never getting an Oscar.

Back when I was young, I thought I was good. I thought I would one day be great. I have learned since then that I have gotten to the peak of my talent. I don't have untapped depths. In fact, the one serious film I did was awful. The *NY Times* review said I walked through every scene with the emotional connection of an autistic kid on crack. Which was definitely an insult to autistic kids. They just weren't wrong. I tried to watch it after. I remembered all the rehearsal, all the time I spent trying to do the method. I spent hours sitting in the park trying to cry for my lost love, but all that really happened was that I got a sore ass. Not sure how people sleep on park benches when sitting on them is slow torture.

So yeah, we live, we learn. My oldest daughter Megan is a vegan, so she stopped talking to me when I went carnivore. Honestly, she had stopped talking to me so many times before that I wasn't too worried. She's living in some town in Northern California with lots of trees. The photos she used to send... it looked pretty. Anyway, I figured she'd send me a text at some point asking for some money like normal. But she didn't. My lawyer tells me she stopped taking her allowance too... so I had him reach out to my ex-wife Norma.

Norma hates me, so I didn't call myself. It's been seventeen years since we've spoken, so maybe she's forgiven me, but I doubt it. Not that Norma doesn't have reason to hate me. Actually, if I were her, I would hate me. We started dating in high school, and we made plans to be together forever. Because at eighteen forever is something that feels real. Now at 52 life seems both shorter and longer than I could have ever imagined.

My biographer wrote that she got pregnant on prom night, but honestly, that's just a cute click-bait heading. In reality, she was pregnant before prom ever came around, dragging herself to school, so stomach sick, wearing my big black hoody. We both graduated, for which my mother was immensely grateful, and we got married in the courthouse the week summer break started. She had moved in with me and my mom back then and she was working in the Piggly Wiggly with my mom. I think she and my mom were always closer than my mom and I were.

Mom was beautiful and young then. She'd had me at sixteen, and between being poor and working hard on her feet every day, she'd never lost her figure. I remember she'd leave the house just before I left for school each morning, with her hair up in a bouffant and her red lipstick, already smiling in her "Thank you for shopping with us" way, her white apron tied up to show off her figure.

In my defense, I never meant to leave Watertown. Never thought I would, not really. It wasn't like I had a plan. Sure, I went to Syracuse for the audition, but it wasn't like I thought I'd get it. The touring show's lead had been in a car accident and I got the part. You've probably read about it already. "Broken Legs is Lucky Break for Future Star." The plan was I would tour for three months with the company and be back in Watertown for the birth.

It's not my fault they picked me for the movie version. I invited Norma to come to Hollywood with me, but she was eight months along and scared to leave home. Wanted her family around for the birth. And yeah, I promised to be there when the baby was born. And I planned to. It wasn't my fault she came a week early. I got there when they were both still in hospital. Norma had changed. The little whiny pink thing in her arms was more important than me. Even my mom was more interested in the baby than she was about me telling her how the shoot was going.

After the movie, I went back, and we tried. Well, Norma tried to make us a house and a home and a family unit, but now I can see she was right. I was spending all my time doing interviews and flying around promoting the movie and I wasn't there for her, or for Megan. And once I'd been everywhere, Watertown just seemed too small, too boring, too... well, it didn't fit whom I was becoming. I told Mom and her I wanted to move to Hollywood with them, but neither of them wanted to go. My mom could have been a movie star even then. She was so pretty, but she was happy being the queen of Watertown, and she knew more than me about how fleeting fame and success could be. I bought her a house, probably the only good thing I've ever really done in my life, within walking distance to town, and she retired from Piggly Wiggly but kept up with the girls she worked with on her bridge nights. Norma came with me to LA. To a luxury suite in a hotel where she and the baby spent all their time while I started work on the next film and went to social events to promote myself and the film.

She was finished with me long before she knew I'd cheated. The biographer said she stormed out after she found red lipstick in my car; he said I'd begged her to stay, that it had only been the one time. But the truth was, I was sleeping with more people than Kevin Bacon and she knew it. She didn't fight or scream. Just one day I came home after being gone a few days and the room didn't smell like dirty diapers and milk. She was gone.

She invited me to Megan's things at the beginning—birthday parties and school graduations. And then one day she just stopped bothering. I think I had missed a birthday. In all fairness, I think my assistant sent a gift, but I hadn't showed up. So then I would see Megan if I went to visit mom. Megan would come over to grandma's and I'd take her shopping. My career was going pretty well then, and I didn't get home as often as I should have. Mom was looking older and older each time I got there. She'd gone from a brunette to a bottle ash-blonde. Easier to hide the gray, I guess. And I was married to Karin, or was it Amiee at that point, and Megan would come out to LA once a year and stay with me and whatever wife and children were at the house then?

So in hindsight, I wasn't a great dad, but I gave her everything she ever asked for. Her mom never had to work, even though she did, and well, like I said, it wasn't my fault. But I tried. I tried with her, and the rest of the kids... well, at least the ones I knew about. I mean, I paid for all of them, didn't I? It wasn't like I'd planned to have any of them or been consulted by most of the mothers.

Priscilla was the wife that lasted the longest. She and I hooked up on set of the first of the Crash Race movies. Come on, you know you've seen at least one of the series. They are fun; lots of thrills and no real plot to get in the way of the action. Someone once said my films were like popcorn—you liked them while they were on but in the end you didn't remember anything much about them and you were still hungry for something better. There are worse things than being popcorn.

It was the peak of her career to be in the film, and I think she thought marrying me would help her career more. Funny thing is she's a better actress than me, but I get cast more than she does.

Anyway, it was during the second Crash Race movie that I realized I hated eating meat and salt and water. I mean, the diet had worked well enough to get me through the first film, but I felt nothing when I ate. It was just a task necessary to live. And then one day I realized meat was so much better served rare. Ok, so I should have known this already, but I grew up with a mother who made sure the meat was brown all the way through before it hit the plate. So I'd just always ordered everything well done. And now that meat was all I ate and there was no sauce to drown it, dry, burned-up meat was just nasty. I was at some nice steak house talking to a producer about a film and he said, "Let me order for you," and well, you can't say no to that. So he ordered two rare steaks, asparagus, and a bottle of red wine. The steak was a revelation. It was soft and tender and juicy. The blood pouring down my throat felt more invigorating than the red wine I followed it with.

And after that, all I ate was rare meat. I realized I really only liked the taste of the blood. That's when I started blending raw steaks for breakfast.

This was when Prisilla left. When she walked in on me drinking a raw filet mignon from the magic bullet. Somehow, this crossed a line that screwing her best friend in the hot tub in front of the security cameras hadn't. But women are crazy.

I never felt so great. My body looked like it hadn't looked in 20 years and I had so much energy. And then came the accident on set.

I was playing this scene where they had me strapped in a chair and a woman was threatening me with a baton, and it was supposed to be a little scary and a little raunchy, like I was supposed to pretend it was sexual. Anyway, I leaned back and boom, the chair tipped backwards.

Now, this isn't the kind of thing they are going to advertise on the movie poster. Star gets concussion while tied to a chair. But anyway, the next thing you know, I wake up in a hospital. And I have a pain in my head so bad I want to rip my damn head off. And they give me all these drugs and the pain goes down, but... well, there's brain fog and I feel so goddamn off. So then they take me back in and find out there's a brain bleed. Three weeks off the shoot while they opened my scalp and the guys in post had to fix it so no one saw the part of my head they had to shave. And I was back at work. But all that energy, all the looking great and feeling great, well, that was shot to hell. In the hospital they'd served me all this awful carb-filled food and I came out looking like the marshmallow man from ghostbusters.

So I went back to eating raw meat smoothies, but it just didn't feel like enough. I was always hungry. So I got my assistant to ask the butcher if there was a way to get blood, you know, from the slaughter-house. And it turned out it can be done. I started feeling better. And it turned out the younger the animal, the more energy I got from it, you know. So lambs' blood is way yummier and energy-giving than sheep's blood. Ditto for calves and cows.

It was hard to get back in the shape I'd been but I worked hard at it. With Priscilla out of the house, there were no distractions. But the brain fog was still there. I was afraid even though I was getting my six-pack back I wasn't going to be able to remember the scripts. Then one day I cut my finger on a knife and I stuck my finger in my mouth and it tasted amazing.

So you know what happened next. Priscilla called you, didn't she? I mean, someone had to have ratted me out. You know it's my own kid. I have custody. Well, joint custody. She found the hole in the sole of the baby's foot, didn't she? You have no idea how much better I felt. I didn't take much. I wasn't going to kill him, for Christ's sake. I was just trying to be healthy. It's just like that bitch to call the police. It's not fair, you know. I didn't really do anything wrong; I was just trying to stay young and healthy enough to keep working. I was just sticking to my diet.

Chapter 14

Disappearing

*V*ampires, it is said, cannot leave reflections in mirrors. But they certainly can be seen and felt. When the ordinary members of society stop interacting with their fellows the disappearance is more subtle. They become background extras without words. Then cutouts. So yell, wave your arms. Better to be thought mad than not to be thought of at all.

Brenda put her hands under the tap, and the damn thing didn't work. Nothing ever worked anymore. She pulled them out and put the right one under the soap dispenser, and nothing... At least when the toilet hadn't worked, she'd been able to push the button. All she wanted to do was wash her hands. Automation's sole function, she thought, was to make humans more and more dependent and then hopeless when the automation doesn't work.

She pushed the door open and went back to her desk. Not that anyone had noticed she was gone. When you work in a cubicle, you do your best to disappear, and so does everyone around you. No one wants to be that person who is disturbing everyone else. She picked up the next file; another closed loan. Her job was to verify that everything had been done correctly and that the property had been re-conveyed to the borrower. Or if the house had been sold, as was more often the case—because who really paid off their mortgage anymore?—that the house had to be conveyed to the new owner and the new mortgage company. Then whatever was left in the escrow company would be refunded to the borrower.

Pretty basic stuff. Really, just a bunch of paperwork. She was pretty convinced that in the next year or so they would invent an AI to do the whole process, and she and every other person in a cubicle on floors 9 and 8 would be out of a job. She was sure the guys at the executive suites on floor 12 would be more than happy to cut all their jobs and not have to pay them. The floors below them were empty now. She remembered when those floors had been filled with customer service agents, until they'd outsourced all of them to call centers in India. The landlord had been trying to rent them out again, but no one wanted commercial property after the pandemic. She'd worked from home for almost a year. It had been nice to be home at first, but she'd looked forward to getting out of the house and seeing other people. She'd thought it would be nice to go to lunch with her co-workers and celebrate birthdays in the lunchroom and just have people to talk to. But when she got back, everyone was so much more shut off than they used to be. Or maybe it was just her in her mask, covering her expressions and her reluctance to stand too close to anyone. She felt like she was invisible.

She went back to her desk and her phone rang. She went to grab for it but she saw "potential spam" and sent it to voicemail. It didn't seem like anyone called anymore. Just texts occasionally from good friends, or going on social media to discover everyone but you was having a great life, had flawless skin, and was succeeding at everything they had ever tried. She couldn't be bothered after years of being on Facebook. She quit all of it—Facebook, Instagram, anything where people took photos of uneaten food in restaurants or tried to sell her anything. She'd gone back to watching TV. Not streaming, because she wanted to be surprised by what was coming. Because she wanted to be bored by the commercials and appalled by the news. She wanted to feel something. Lately she'd just started to feel so disconnected that not only was she invisible to others, but the world itself was stepping away from her. It was a strange sensation, and she wanted to watch the news and see the horror of politics and war just to feel connected to something, even if that something was outrage.

She clocked off on time and walked out with everyone, nodding to them as she walked out. This was her new thing. Back in the day, she used to do the half-smile to acknowledge other people. It seemed like it was enough to just lift the corners of her mouth while keeping her mouth closed and her teeth covered. Just a quick, deliberate action to let those around her know she was saying hi without having to say hi. It was like that episode of Seinfeld; she felt if she started saying hi to everyone she would stand out, and then people would expect it from her, and then one day when she was just too tired to be bothered to say hi they would think she hated them and the war of silent sulking would start. So she didn't risk the hi. Instead, she had always done the slightly painful, insincere smile. And now, with COVID and the K95 mask cutting into her checks, she couldn't do that anymore. So she stood in her cubicle, put on her coat, grabbed her purse and could see James in the cubicle next door standing as well. She nodded at him, pulling her chin down, then she turned to grab her phone off the desk and put it in her purse. The computer had shut down, and she felt like she was forgetting something, but she couldn't remember what it might be.

She stepped out of her cubicle and could see her boss still in his office on the phone. She nodded, and he didn't acknowledge her, but he was deeply engrossed in the call with his wife about what color carpet they would put in their new house.

She nodded to June in Accounting as she walked past her cubicle. June always stayed late, then she shuffled out behind the other people before leaving. She was glad she didn't know any of them well enough to have to talk to them, or even nod. She was starting to feel like a bobblehead doll.

The elevator was open, and she walked in. Two burly men walked in behind her and didn't seem to notice her at all. She had to squeeze out into the corner so they wouldn't knock into her. They were having a heated discussion on the use of the red card during the rugby world cup. She had no idea what on earth they were talking about, but arms were flying; it was passionate. She wished she felt passionate about anything. Their voices filled the small space even while other people filled all the rest of the space.

The freeway was much as it always was. Cars didn't seem to see her, to see her car, and tried to switch lanes right into her, but she just braked and let them in. It wasn't worth the road rage, or the paint damage. No one was getting home before anyone else. The freeway was always going to be slow and painful, and she just wasn't arrogant enough to ignore that fact. Whether you drove a used Hyundai or a new Lexus, no one got there any faster than the guys in front of them. Still, she remembered a time when people at least gave you a space in front of your car. Since the pandemic, everyone wanted to always cut ahead to that little space she left in front. Seemed like people were driving worse, playing more with their cellphones, stoned on prescriptions or pot, their clouds of vape juice shooting out of their open windows.

She drove into her parking garage without having an accident and dragged herself out of her car. Her neighbor had driven in before her and had followed her through the metal gate. Their parking spot was closer to the gate, and they were out and on their way to the elevator before she reached her parking spot. She pulled in and sighed. Another night home alone with the cat. Maybe she'd order a pizza, but there were still leftovers from yesterday to eat.

She pulled herself out of the car and leaned in to grab her coat and purse. No point in hurrying. The elevator wouldn't be back down again yet. She walked slowly to the elevator and hit the button. It took a minute to come down while she tried to remember the name of the neighbor who had gone up before her—Christie... something. She'd seen her at an HOA meeting. Or was it Susan? They'd passed each other so many times going back and forth and up and down the elevator, but she felt like they'd never met. It was probably her fault. Instead of just fading into the background, she should try to start a conversation, she thought. Or at least find out her name. If the place burned down tomorrow, she wouldn't know to tell the firemen where exactly she lived. If the place burned down tomorrow, no one would probably know who she was. She'd lived in the building for eight years. Eight years she counted in her head, eight years of passing people on the elevator and in the halls, smiling that blank smile you smile at strangers. Eight years of making comments about the weather that filed the silence and said nothing. Eight years of living an invisible life in the same apartment, eight years of driving every day to the same job in the same building. And tomorrow, if her job was gone, what then? How would she pay the rent on this apartment?

The elevator opened with a grinding sound and she hopped in alone, pushing the button for the third floor. The elevator had been fashionable when it was installed in the early 70s, with fake plastic wood panels and an orange linoleum floor. No one had spent money on the elevator since installation and the floor was now almost as brown as the walls. The elevator swayed as it slowly ascended, a low hum with a grinding noise, even now, quietly in the background. The thought crossed her mind that the elevator may be broken. Not the kind of broken that would require a technician and everyone in the building hauling their laundry from the laundry room up the stairs for a week but the kind of broken where at any moment the wire, or chain, or prayer, or whatever was holding her up was failing and she was about to fall to her death screaming in a small metal box with terrible fake plastic wood paneling.

And then the metal death box stopped. Was this it, she wondered? Who would mourn me if I were gone? She had no ties left to family since her mother had died, and she wasn't even sure whom the state would notify of her death. She held her breath for an instant that seemed like an eternity. Finally the door opened.

It ground its way open on her floor just like it was supposed to do and she hopped out a little faster than necessary.

She walked slowly down the hallway, looking at the formerly cream carpet beneath her feet and the dark green Laura Ashley striped wallpaper on the walls with the tiny candle sconces that made the entire poorly lit hallway seem like a set from a 1950s monster feature. She opened the door to her apartment and was greeted by darkness and quiet. She had thought about getting a cat, just something alive to welcome her home when she got back from work, but it didn't seem fair to trap an animal into a life of solitude even more extensive than her own. When she retired, when she was home all the time, she would get an animal then. Maybe one of those corgi crosses she'd seen on Facebook.

She put away her shoes and hung up her jacket, ready to put them on again the following day.

And the next day, and the next day, and the next. It was on a Friday that she finally realized.

She walked into the bathroom and her shoulder hit June's from Accounting. Brenda apologized. "So sorry, June." June took a step back, rubbed her shoulder, but did not respond. "So sorry," Brenda said again, but June said nothing. June just flinched and kept walking. Brenda stepped to the side, hurt. What she had done was an accident. Why didn't June accept her apology?

Brenda went to wash her hands, and the water didn't work. She went to get soap. And the soap dispenser gave her nothing. And she sighed and looked up into the mirror. It was at that moment she saw what others already knew. She was invisible. She looked down at her hands. She could see them, but when she put them in front of the mirror, there was no reflection.

Brenda Ann Smith, after years of being an invisible cog in the machine of existence, had disappeared.

She ran screaming out of the bathroom, waving her arms in front of other people's faces, in front of James and her boss. No one saw her again.

Chapter 15

Remember Me

When the brain or body are torn, the accepted wisdom is that the rest of the senses or physical abilities will compensate. Braille, limb replacement, canes, wheelchairs, mental health therapy, seeing-eye dogs, pills and injections.

But what about the subtle failures of the brain? And what happens when they tell you it's 'incurable'? No chance. Nothing you can do. Or is there? For there is a world of dreams that just may bring an answer.

I woke up aching, the pain in my arm the most intense, a fiery hot pain that poured up into my shoulder and skull, then trickled down my back to join the ache that filled every cell. I didn't know why I hurt so badly, or what had happened. Later I would be told. Later than that I would remember. Waking up, I couldn't open my eyes or move. I could only feel. I could feel the pain. I don't know if the doctors knew I was awake then, or if my vitals spiked, but the medication took me down again and I was unconscious—not asleep, not resting, just not screaming. The pain was over for the moment.

The next time I woke up, it was as if I were flying. I couldn't feel my body, but my eyes were open, and I could see. "How are you feeling, David?" asked a white-coated man leaning over me.

"What happened?"

The white-coated man, a doctor I guessed, leaned in to look in my eye. "You were in an accident, David. Do you remember it?"

"No. Am I paralyzed?" I asked, terrified now that the numbness I felt was paralysis. That somehow the absence of pain was the end result of my nerves dying.

"No, David."

"Everyone calls me Dave," I said reflectively, because the way he said David made me feel I was back in high school in front of the principal. And I wasn't sure he wasn't lying. I felt paralyzed, or at least wrong. "I can't feel my hands," I said, lifting one slightly off the bed. I could lift it, but I couldn't feel it. "What happened?"

"We have you heavily medicated, Dave. You have a lot of broken bones and were in a coma."

"How long?"

"Not long. A couple of days. The important thing now is that you rest. I'm Doctor Scott and I'll be in to see you again later."

I slowly made a fist. I couldn't feel it, but I could see my hand closing, my fingers going back and forth. The doctor said I'd be ok. What was his name? Doctor Scott. "Ok," I said to the doctor as he walked to the end of the bed, made a note on the chart, and walked out.

I drifted in and out for the next couple of days. The nurses came in looking like one person, all sweet and neat and firm, taking blood and reading vitals, never letting me sleep longer than a few hours before the next donation was needed. More blood, more numbers for the chart, more morphine. Morphine was my friend.

My mom was the first visitor, crying, blowing snot in a tissue at the sight of my face. I didn't recognize her at first with her face in a mask. "Oh, Davey," she said in the same voice she used when I fell off the swing in kindergarten. I recognized her voice, that same voice I'd been listening to since before I was born. "Oh, Davey," she'd say when she was sad. "Oh, Davey," she'd say when she was angry. "Oh, Davey," she'd say when she was proud. She wasn't proud often. It was hard to please her, although honestly, I had tried.

She hated it when I bought my motorbike. It was not the only thing she'd hated over the years, but it was definitely near the top of the list. And now the "Oh, Davey" said "I told you so. If you had only listened to me. Motorcycles are dangerous. What were you thinking?" And I deserved this one.

I was obviously too old to become a biker. My friend Mikey called it a midlife crisis, but I think of it as more of an end-of-life crisis. The kids went to college and then found jobs and partners so far away. It was just me and Maria and I really blew it. Just because you can, it doesn't mean you should. I guess in my head I was always 21, and without the kids to ground me I behaved badly. And Maria left.

So my life ended. And I bought the motorbike.

"Oh, Davey," my mother said again. "You have no idea what this did to me. I can't have shocks like this at my age."

I opened my eyes to look at her. She'd pulled down the mask and there was an old woman, her hair neatly dyed blonde and set in an updo, and her lipstick was slightly smudged over the edge of her thin lips and on one of her front teeth. And I didn't recognize her at all. I knew she was my mother from the way her hair looked, the smell of Chanel No. 5 she'd always worn, the bend of her shoulders, and the voice, that voice. But I didn't see her and recognize her. And I wondered when the last time I'd really stopped to look at her had been.

I saw her all the time, but I'd stopped looking. Why look at the decay of the most glamorous woman I had ever met?

She was the mother all the other boys fantasied about, the mother who embarrassed me by wearing button-up shirts with gold chains that swung between her breasts. Breasts that all the other boys talked about when she was young, when I was young. Her breasts had shriveled and so had her neck and her cheeks. I looked at her hands. They were withered, with sunspots. How didn't I know this? How didn't I recognize her?

She stayed with me for four hours that first day. By the time she left, I felt like I knew her face. It's a strange thing. Then, as she was leaving, she said, "The police are investigating the crash."

"The accident?"

"They think it might not be an accident, dear. The doctor told them you were well enough to talk to and they are going to be in tomorrow."

"Not an accident?" My head spun. I still couldn't remember anything about the accident. "How do you know this, Mom?"

"Well, they needed permission to examine your bike, and since you were unconscious, I gave it to them."

"You did?"

"Well, yes. The bike was brought to my place after the accident. You still had my address on your driver's license."

I started to remember. When Maria kicked me out, I'd moved to my mom's house. How long had I lived there? A month or two, until I'd found an apartment, but I hadn't changed my address. Rather than face the DMV, my permanent address was Mom's place.

I had a new apartment in the Valley, but I hadn't changed the address, or really ever unpacked or decorated. There was a bed, and clothes on the floor in a box or two. I remembered thinking that I didn't want to unpack. I didn't really want to believe our marriage was over. Somewhere in my mind, I still wanted to be back with Maria.

Why could I remember that but not the accident, or the lines on my mother's cheeks?

I reached up to scratch my head and hit a bandage. "Why is my head bandaged?"

"Oh, Davey," said my mother, almost tearing up. "Don't make me go through it all. You know you hit the ground and your skull cracked. I mean, I thought I was going to lose you. You have no idea how hard it's all been."

"My skull cracked... and broken arm and ribs, and what else—"

"You expect me to be able to keep track of it all? It's a wonder you're alive at all. I told you not to buy that stupid motorbike. I mean, if you hadn't been on that bike, that car couldn't have hit you."

"A car hit me?"

"Yes, of course, dear. The police are looking for more witnesses."

"More witnesses?"

"Yes. There's one, of course, the guy who called 911. But you know, more witnesses. They know the car was following you, then pulled out next to you, and what the witness says is they then deliberately pulled back into you, throwing you off the road."

"I can't remember any of this," I said, suddenly terrified. How much had I lost that I couldn't even remember getting run off the road, and who would want to do that, anyway?

My mother stood to leave. Now that she'd dropped the bomb, she was more than happy to escape the blast zone. She stood smiling as if she'd just told me the weather was fine. "I need to get home, dear. Almost time to feed the dog. I'll be here tomorrow." She leaned down to peck me on the cheek and missed and pecked the end of my nose instead, and I knew from the way it felt that she'd smeared her cheap red lipstick all over the tip of my nose. I sighed as she dragged her coat from behind the chair she had been sitting on.

The doctor came in the next morning on the regularly scheduled round. And I was waiting for him. The nurse, whom I didn't recognize but there were so many of them, told me that my doctor would be by at 9 a.m. Doctor Scott. "Is that the doctor that I saw yesterday?" I asked.

"Yes, indeed. He's been your physician since you arrived." I tried to form a picture of him in my head, but as far as I got was a white coat, brown hair.

At 9 a.m. a man in a white coat with brown hair arrived in my room and I did not recognize him at all.

"Hi. You're looking better today." He grabbed my chart and looked over it. "Looks like everything is mending as expected. Do you remember the accident yet?"

"No, I don't remember the accident, or just before it... and," I said, realizing it was true now that the words were coming out of my mouth, "I don't remember you. I mean, I know you were here yesterday and the nurse said your name is Dr. Scott, but I don't recognize you."

"Interesting," he said, walking around to the side of the bed and coming up close to me. He looked at me with renewed interest, and I found it somewhat terrifying. What had I said? What was he thinking? "Is it just me?"

"No. I have recognized none of the nurses. I mean, maybe every one is different, but I didn't recognize my mother until she started to talk. I mean... well..."

He pulled out his little light. "Let me check this," he said, checking my pupils for signs of concussion. "Very interesting. If you don't mind, I think we are going to need to do an MRI and see what's going on."

They say an MRI is non-invasive, but that's only because they've never been in one. The sound invaded my brain and made my eyeballs shake. All I wanted to do was get out of the hellish metal tube and back to my quiet hospital bed. And you know, if it was making the hospital bed seem like a place I wanted to be, there was nothing about it that was good.

It was after a barely edible meal of gray meat-type substance with grayer sauce and a side of mostly rehydrated potatoes and greenish beans that the doctor came back in. I assumed it was the same doctor, because who else would come in giddy, with a huge smile on his face?

"What's up, Doc?" The doctor did not see the humor in this. And he sat down on the side of the bed.

"So, Dave, did you recognize me as I came in?"

"No, Doc, just know you're wandering around in a white coat and a nice shirt underneath, so you're a doctor."

"Well, I have sent your file on to the neurology department—"

"What the hell, don't tell me I have a brain tumor—"

"No, Dave. They confirmed what I suspected. You have acquired prosopagnosia, or as it's sometimes referred to, face blindness."

"Face blind... Doc, I can see you just fine."

"Yes, well, the MRI confirmed my diagnosis. You have received damage in the inferior occipital lobe at the fusiform gyrus."

"Doc, I don't know what the hell you are talking about."

He looked down in the way that doctors do when they want to tell you the worst news ever and they would prefer to say it to the floor. "You have some damage to your brain as a result of the accident and it has damaged the part of your brain that processes facial recognition."

"So I won't be able to recognize anyone ever again?"

"Well, it's not as simple as that. We don't know for sure. There is still a lot of swelling in the brain, but nothing that needs surgery. Some or all of the function may return, or it may not."

"Doc," I sat up, "how the hell am I supposed to function if everyone is a stranger all the time?"

"There are people born with the condition and they have found methods to work around it, like recognizing hair, or posture, or people's voice. But like I said, the function may return. You still can't remember the accident, can you?"

"Nope." Although I felt like it was coming back, like I could feel it just out there, just out of touch. A dream half-remembered, and I reached for it, but nothing came.

"Well, we fully expect that memory will come back. There is no obvious damage in any of the core memory centers in the brain, but these things take time."

I stared at the doctor's face, trying to frame a picture of it in my mind for later. He had a mole on the side of his nose. I would remember that. If a guy in a white shirt walks in with a mole on the side of his nose, he is Dr. Scott. I said this to myself while I said to him, "You really don't have the answers, do you?"

"No," he said, coloring slightly, and the mole stood out even more against his slight flush.

There was a knock on the open door of the hospital room. It was the police. The doctor looked up at them and nodded, then nodded at me, glad to get a reprieve and resume his rounds. One had to wonder, do doctors really walk around the whole time or do they go see three or four people a day then hide in an office the rest of the time while the nurses do all the actual work?

"Mr. David Little?" asked a male uniformed cop.

"Yep," I said, and he and a female in plain clothes, obviously a cop, walked in. It was funny how I knew that she was a cop despite not wearing a uniform. Not that I could from one moment to the next tell you anything about either of them. I couldn't pick them out of a lineup, but I knew he was the beat cop and she was the detective. It's amazing what television had taught me.

"Do you mind if we ask you some questions?" she asked, pulling up a chair while the uniform stood at the door like her bodyguard.

"Sure." Anything to kill the time. The skin under my cast was starting to itch, and I could feel the pain meds start to wear off in the low aching in my face and chest.

"What do you remember of the accident, Mr. Little?"

"Please call me Dave."

She smiled slightly. "Dave." I looked at her. She was cute, button nose, amber skin. It was odd to realize that as much as I stared at her face, as soon as she was gone, I wouldn't remember her.

"I was hoping you'd be able to answer some questions about the incident." She looked down at her notes. "You were on Sierra Highway."

"Yes, going east."

"Yes. The report we have is that a late-model gray sedan was following you, then sped up beside you and swung their vehicle for you, hitting you off the road and down an embankment."

I tried to picture this. I remembered driving east. I had left Maria's house. I was on my way back to my place. I remembered her being angry at me. I'd gone to her house to try to beg her to come back. I don't know what I'd been thinking. I'd walked in without telling her I was coming.

"Do you know anyone, sir, who may wish you harm?"

"No," I said, thinking of Maria.

She'd come at me with such a look. "How dare you? How dare you cheat on me, then the minute you get sad because you're alone, you decide to just swing by the house you've forced your wife to move into? You son of a—" I had known what the next words were even as I ran back down the stairs towards the bike.

"Sir, do you know anyone who owns a late-model gray sedan?"

"Doesn't everyone own a late-model gray sedan?" I asked. I had owned one myself. I'd called her Betsy, which annoyed Maria. I think it especially annoyed her when she got the car in the settlement and I'd cried that I'd just lost my best girl Betsy. I was at that point in the divorce proceedings where annoying her was giving me pleasure. And I wasn't paying for an attorney, she was, so I let her spend her money being annoyed with me. Actually, come to think of it, I don't think I'd ever found Betsy's pink slip and signed it over. Maria may have Betsy, but she was still mine on paper.

"Where were you coming from the night of the attempted murder?"

"Attempted murder?" I said. "Is that what you are calling this?"

"Yes, sir. It seems clear that there was an attempt made on your life."

"Oh, shit," I said as it hit home. I wasn't in the hospital because my fat ass couldn't keep my bike on the road. I was in the hospital because someone wanted me dead. Who would possibly want me dead?

"Sir, do you remember anything about the incident?"

I shook my head, wishing I did. The doc said my memories would return, didn't he? Maybe with time.

"Maybe I'll remember more later. I don't know."

"Sir, do you mind if we leave these photos here with you? If you remember anything at all, here is my number. Just give me a call and leave me a message twenty-four hours a day."

I took the card and touched her fingers. A pretty girl was giving me a way to call her twenty-four hours a day, and I was in too much of a flat panic to even think about it. Someone had tried to kill me. I waited till the cute police chick had left and her face had faded from my mind and then I started to sob. Someone wanted to kill me.

That night I had the first dream. I dreamed the whole accident. It was as if I was reliving it; just riding on my bike and then a screeching of wheels, and I turned and looked and the gray car was headed towards me. I couldn't see the driver's face. It was a blur, but the car hit me, and I flew. And then, as I was falling toward the earth, I woke up screaming.

"Can I come in?" I looked up. I knew that voice. I didn't recognize her face. I wasn't sure if she'd always had her hair like that.

"Remember me?" she asked inquisitively. She knew I couldn't see faces. Someone had told her.

"Maria, of course."

"I thought you wouldn't recognize me."

"I know you."

She came in, her head down. "I am so sorry. I heard what happened. Your mom tells me that you can't remember the accident, and that you have some kind of brain damage."

Trust my mother to ring my ex-wife and tell her I'm in the hospital and a head case.

"Yeah, the cops just told me that someone drove me off the road." She pulled up a chair and sat by the edge of the bed, not too close, just closer than we had been in a long time.

"Your mom says you can't see faces anymore," she said. "I didn't know if you would remember me."

"I can see them. I just can't catch a picture of them in my head. It's hard to explain. It's not like I look at you right now and I don't see that you have a face."

"Your mom says it's permanent." Maria looked concerned. I knew that much. I was studying her face more now than I ever had when we were married, and I thought I knew what she looked like.

"Well, since she's told you everything, I'm not sure there's that much more for me to say. They say that I might remember the accident, but that I'm never going to remember a face again."

"How did you know it was me?"

"Your voice. I would know your voice anywhere."

She smiled a slow, sad smile. "Well, I just wanted to stop by and make sure you were all right."

"Thanks, Maria. You know I'm sorry. I am so very sorry for everything I have ever done to hurt you. I have had a lot of time to think about what's important and I just wanted to let you know that."

"I'm sorry too, Dave. I don't even know why I'm here. I just wanted to see you and see if you were ok. Your mom made it sound like you were on death's doorstep."

"I got lucky. I should have been. It's good to see you."

"It's good to see you too. Will you remember that I've been here?"

"Sure. I just won't remember your face. Are you doing your hair different?"

"It's longer."

"It's been too long since we split, Maria. I have missed you." I felt tears dripping from my eyes and I reached up to touch them. I couldn't remember doing that before. I wasn't sure what was wrong. "Sorry," I said, pushing them away, "they still have me on a lot of medication."

She touched my arm. "Bye, Dave. I'd better go. You get better, ok?"

"Yeah." I nodded, and she walked away, and my eyes started to weep. It was completely out of my control. My brain was obviously broken, and I didn't know what else had gone wrong. It was nice to see Maria, but my left leg was itching insanely and I couldn't reach it or do anything about it. I hit the bell for the nurse and hoped she'd be able to get me some tissues to dry my eyes.

As I felt better, the time in hospital seemed to become slower and slower. With longer intervals between doctor's visits. I wanted the nurse to come take my blood just to fill the endless emptiness that streaming TV shows and reading books I wasn't interested in couldn't.

Even sleeping wasn't a release. I'd started to dream more now that they were filling me with fewer drugs. And every night it was the same dream, or memory, trying to surface. I was on my bike and suddenly I was flying through the air. Every night I woke up screaming, falling back towards the earth.

They released me with my leg still in a cast and my chest still taped up and I moved, as one wants to in their middle age, back in with my mother.

She picked me up in her car. It was a late-model gray sedan too, a Honda Civic, and I wondered if the police had any leads at all. The orderly pushed the passenger's seat back as far as he could and helped me and my crutch get in. I was going to have to get myself out, so that was going to be fun. My mom went around to the driver's side and climbed in, her updo just barely visible over the steering wheel. She then proceeded to drive off in a way that made me think I would have been safer driving my mangled motorbike home.

She swerved from one lane to the next, talking with her hands while blaming other drivers for being in her path. "Get out of my way, you idiot. Davey, you know you can stay as long as you like, but I don't have time to nurse you. What do you think you're doing?" she said, screeching on the brakes. "If you're going to pull over, indicate. Like I said, I have a very busy schedule, so you'll need to look after yourself, you know. I mean, I'll bring you home food if you want.

"Look where you're going! Can you believe people these days? I mean, if he wanted to pull in, he should have looked. I'm going to see if Maria can look in on you. And you'll need to keep the place tidy. I don't want you leaving anything lying about." She turned the wheel and jumped the curb up to the driveway in front of her condo. I peeled my fingers off the handle I had been holding on to for dear life.

"Can you get yourself out of the car, dear? I need to check the mailbox. I'll meet you at the house. I'm going to have to find some sheets for the spare bed. I am not sure if I left it made that last time." She walked off, possibly still talking to herself, and I wedged myself out of the car and onto my crutch. Then I pushed the door closed and hobbled to the front of the car. There was a ding on the front of the car, like she'd hit something. Almost like she'd hit me and I'd bounced off. But surely anyone who had that kind of damage on their car would have had their car fixed by now. Now that the police were investigating, wouldn't it be a good idea to go to a body shop and get rid of the evidence? Or maybe that would just be suspicious. Maybe all the body shops would be monitored.

Maybe if you'd just hit a person, the best idea would be to go hit a building or another car and then your insurance would pay for the bodywork and the evidence would be gone. Or sell the car. The police must know all this. The police would be investigating.

"Mom," I said over the KFC she'd brought home. "The police called today. They want to come tomorrow to talk to me."

"Fine, but I hope they don't put their police lights on. You know it doesn't look good if there are cops sitting with their lights blaring in the driveway. Actually, can you go see them in their office instead?"

I shook my head and pointed to my leg. "I can't drive. They need to come here."

"I could drive you."

I quaked at the thought. "It's all set up for them to come here."

When I opened the door to the cops, I was saddened to see the cute detective wasn't there. It wasn't until she got in and sat down that I realized it was the same woman, but she hadn't put any makeup on that morning and her hair was up. I found myself looking harder, and didn't recognize her voice, but her face said that she knew me and I had to assume she did.

"Mr. Little... sorry, Dave, could we come in?"

I nodded and wandered back to the couch, expecting them to follow and close the door after them since they had two working legs and two working arms. I splatted myself down on the sofa, which is where I'd mostly been since the accident.

"We were just following up to see if you had remembered anything more since the accident," said the detective, sitting herself across from me on the recliner and pulling out her notepad. The uniformed police officer with her stayed standing. I wondered if it were the same one.

"I have been remembering more," I said. "I think I could remember almost the entire day I had almost died. I remember leaving Maria's house. And I remember getting on my bike and driving along the Sierra Highway. Then I remember seeing a gray car in my mirrors. The next thing I remember is the impact and the sensation of flying. I don't remember more than that." I don't remember landing broken on the side of the road. My memory doesn't want to go there, doesn't want to feel that. The screaming in my brain starts before I feel the impact. I am tossed up into the sky and I am looking around for land, looking back at the car that hit me... and nothing.

"What can you tell us about the car?" said the detective.

"All cars look the same these days. It didn't have any identifying marks."

"Think hard. No damage to the bumper or anything else? You couldn't see the driver?"

"Nope. I have thought about it a lot. I have nothing."

The detective shut her notepad. "Please call us if you remember anything else. Hopefully, we get some kind of lead on the case, otherwise we don't have enough evidence to prosecute."

"Ok," I said. It never made any sense, anyway. No one would want to kill me. It must have just been an accident. I tried to stand up.

"Mr. Little, we will show ourselves out." She handed me another card. "Please call me if you remember anything."

She let herself out, and I called my mother. "Hi, Mom."

"Hi, Davey. You're up, are you? I left early this morning. Thought you were going to just sleep the day away."

"We don't all get up at 5 a.m., Mom."

"It's the best time of the day. I worked in the garden, and now I'm out. What do you need?"

"Could you bring me home a coffee and a muffin?"

"I've already been to Starbucks today, in the morning."

I checked my watch: 11 a.m.; it was still the morning but there was no point in arguing about it. "Ok."

"I'm at the Vons getting something for you to eat."

"Oh, ok." It seemed like all she ate these days was breakfast cereal, and she'd made dinner every day I was there. I couldn't complain. She really was trying to look after me. In her own way.

"Do you want lamb chops or pork chops?" She was obviously yelling into her phone, holding it out like an old-fashioned radio in the middle of the supermarket. I could hear the supermarket musak, so cheerful, so boring.

"Either, Mom. Whatever you want to get is fine with me."

"I don't know. I wouldn't have called you if I knew what you wanted to eat."

I didn't bother telling her that she hadn't called me. "Pork chops," I said, guessing they were cheaper. She'd give me the bill when she got home to put the money in her account, and I really didn't care.

"Ok," she said and hung up without saying goodbye, her business done.

I opened my Door Dash app and ordered myself a hot coffee, and a double chocolate muffin and, while I was at it, a roast beef sandwich and an extra iced vanilla latte.

I thought about what the detective had said, and what she hadn't said. Seemed like they were going to give up. Not enough evidence. At least I wasn't dead.

I wanted to talk to someone about it. Obviously not my mom. I thought about calling my friend Larry, but that might start him on a long rant about how useless the police was and how the government knew everything and was secretly running experiments on all of us. Last time we'd talked, he'd asked me how I knew they hadn't put in a tracking device when they'd operated on my brain. I mean, most of the time Larry's just a normal guy. He's not one of those guys at the freeway exit with a sign and an aluminum hat, but other times he makes me wonder if that isn't what his future holds.

I thought about calling the kids, but they had their own lives so far away and I wasn't sure how to start or what to say if they answered. We normally just texted. Calling would make them think I was dying.

So I called the person who had been my best friend for most of the last twenty-five years. Maria. I hoped she'd take my call. I didn't realize how much I wanted her to take my call till she picked up. I let my breath go and said, "Hi, Maria."

"Hi, Dave. How are you doing?"

"I'm out of the hospital."

"That's nice. At your mom's?"

"Yeah, be here at least till I can drive again."

"Any idea how long that will be?"

"Five weeks or so. The police came by today."

"They did?"

"Yeah, but it looks like they are dropping the case."

"Oh."

"Yeah," I said, trying to stick my fingers down the top of my cast and itch. "Not enough evidence. I mean, I remember the accident now, but I don't remember any important details. Like I can't tell them what the person who was driving looked like. And it all happened too fast for me to see the license plate or something."

"Do you think the police are going to be keeping track of body shops?"

"For the car, yeah, I suppose so." I found my attention slipping and started to check my Instagram while she was talking. "I suppose they'd do that and maybe, you know, junk yards. I don't know. I mean, it would be a lot of work keeping track of every body shop in the greater LA area."

"You're right, and they couldn't possibly keep track of one in, say, Phoenix."

"Nope... state lines and all that."

"I was thinking of giving Betsy back to you."

"You were?"

"Yeah. You always liked that car more than I did. I like to be up higher when I drive so I leased a Subaru Crosstrek. We don't owe that much to Betsy, and if you want her back..."

"That would be great," I said, realizing how nice it was to have Maria back, talking to me. "After I can drive..."

"Yeah, after that... Did you mean what you said in the hospital when you said you still loved me?" she asked quietly.

"Yep."

There was silence on the phone. I realized I'd never stopped loving her. But maybe everything I'd done had stopped her from loving me.

"I am so sorry for everything," I said.

She didn't respond, but I could hear crying. I said I love you a couple more times, and I heard her blow her nose and hang up.

That was the beginning. She started to come over. And then we started to screw. But cowboy-style, to avoid my broken ribs and broken leg. It wasn't something we'd done before, but she seemed to like being in control. After a couple weeks of that, my mother had had enough.

"I don't need a house filled with a whole bunch of people. I like living alone. Maria seems to be here more than at her house, so can you please go move in with her already?"

Apparently, my shy mother had already told Maria to take me home and shag me there, so we left a couple of days later. Maria drove her new car. It was cute and small and sunburst orange, so much more like her than the gray sedan ever was.

Maria had lost weight since we'd split. I may not remember her face, but I remembered the way her hips felt in my hands. "How much weight have you lost?" I asked her. "You look great." I looked down at my own belly, which had only gotten softer since I'd been out of the hospital.

She pointed to the pink thing on her wrist. "Since I got the Fitbit, I've been working on getting at least 8,000 steps a day. And..." she didn't finish that thought. She didn't eat when she was stressed. I always ate more. So, after the divorce she'd started to look beautiful, and I was starting to look like my father six months before the heart attack.

"It's worked well for you. Maybe I should get one too," I said, and she smiled.

The next day she bought me one, with a standard black strap, not the custom neon pink strap she'd gotten for herself. And life was good. When they took the cast off my leg, I started physio and Maria gave me the keys for Betsy back. She was in the garage. Betsy looked even better than I remembered. Maria had obviously gotten her cleaned more than I did, and she'd had a few of the scratches taken off. It was good to sit in her again. I even managed to drive myself to physiotherapy and the rest of the doctors.

The only problem was when I left physio, I couldn't find Betsy. Everything I'd read about prosopagnosia said it could make recognizing cars and other inanimate objects harder. And the first time I limped around the parking lot for 10 minutes, trying my key in every gray car door. After that, I started taking a photo of where I'd parked. It would have been easier if Betsy had just been a different color, like Maria's bright orange car. But I was learning to cope; at least that's what the shrink they had me seeing every week told me. In some ways, I felt like I was learning to cope for the first time, both with my mom and as a partner in a relationship. The anger I'd always had seemed to have gone.

Maria was helping me, too. She invited my mom to dinner every Sunday and made a big meal.

"So, Davey," said my mother, moving the food around the plate and pretending to eat it. "When are you going to do the right thing and ask her to marry you?"

"Mom!"

"You know she's the only woman brave enough to put up with you once, let alone twice. You've got kids together, you're going to have grandkids together. Just marry her again already."

"Mom," said Maria in that voice that said "Enough." "Thank you for your opinion."

But I knew my mom was right. And that I should do it right, so a few weeks later I went and bought a diamond ring with small pink tourmalines around it. Pink was her favorite color, just like her new smart watch. I wanted to do this right this time.

So that night I took her to dinner at a nice restaurant, I got down on one knee and proposed. Two waiters had to help me back up, but she said yes and took the ring and put it on.

I was back at work. I didn't explain that I couldn't recognize people anymore and I found it easier to just pretend I could. Smile at everyone, act friendly until I realized whom I was talking to. I was ten minutes into a conversation in the elevator before I realized it was Fred in Accounting, and that was only after he mentioned that his wife and he were still planning the big cruise for their wedding anniversary.

I walked with a cane now, but I was trying to walk a lot, a little more every day. I'd probably always have a slight limp, but I didn't care. I was happy. The only thing was the nightmares that still came. I'd wake screaming, falling towards the earth.

I would wake with Maria holding me.

"Do you remember anything?" she said, because she knew I was remembering the accident. That this dream was my brain's way of processing the trauma. "Faces or anything?"

"No," I said, and I realized that my dreams didn't have faces in them anymore. There were people and I knew who the people were, but images of their actual faces were missing. I didn't even see my own face anymore. Yesterday I'd been startled by my own reflection in a shop window. "No faces. Dr. Scott says they aren't coming back. I just keep having the same dream. I am flying off the bike and heading to the ground. I wake up before I hit."

"My poor darling," she said and decided to take advantage of us both being awake.

I was still getting massive headaches. The doc wasn't sure if those would be permanent or not, but the next day I couldn't get up for work, so I called in sick and went back to sleep. Maria brought me some pain pills and kissed me goodbye. And I dreamed the same dream, but

I knew I was dreaming. I knew I was in a dream and I stood outside myself as I flew and fell. And after I landed, twisted and bleeding, I looked back. I remembered now, looking back at the car that hit me. The gray car that I didn't recognize stopped for a second and I looked for the driver's face, but there was nothing. All I could see was the windshield and someone behind it. The car window dropped open and they rested their arm on the window ledge and looked out at me lying broken on the ground. I couldn't see her face, but a neon pink Fitbit watch band shone in the sunlight.

About the Author

I love stories about normal people who find themselves in unexpected situations, whether that is because the world just ended, or because they have just moved to a new planet. I like to explore human limitations even while the human in question no longer has a body or was never human to start with.

I believe that Speculative Fiction has been one of the driving forces of this modern era making us reach for the next great advance. And yes, I am still waiting for my flying car, so to all of you guys with better science skills than me, hurry it up, please. Stories can make us think of all the possibilities and consider what future we want to build.

I always enjoy a story that surprises me and tests my view of reality. I hope you do too and will appreciate my offerings to the gods of speculation.

For more information about upcoming releases sign up for my newsletter at www.sawooderson.com

Acknowledgement

I'd like to thank Richard Mueller for writing the pithy forwards you find at the beginning of each story.

Richard is a friend and a mentor. His works span, television, film and print.

His contribution to this book was invaluable. You will find Richard's catalog of books at GoodReads or at Amazon.

***

I would also like to acknowledge Mickey, without whom I would not have the time to vent these little nightmares out into the world.

It is to him I dedicate this book.

Also By S.A. Wooderson

For more disturbing little stories please click on one of the books below.

To find out the newest releases and news please join my newsletter.

Future Sins Volume One

Stories of our deadly sins: Greed. Envy. Wrath. Sloth.

Technological advancement has not led us to overcome our basic human flaws but helped carry them into the future.

These short stories will challenge your view of what it means to be human and keep you up at night wondering what comes next.

Future Sins Volume Two

Future Sins Volume Two crawls out of the gate with two tales of Sloth, one in which belief and science battle for the soul of a young man and the future of humanity and another where a different young man discovers a secret hidden in plain sight. Lust delves into the possibilities of love and sex in different alternate realities. Gluttony is a desire impossible to satisfy, whether it is seeking something new and untried or just trying to mine the most minerals possible. Meanwhile, Pride comes before a fall and Jacob Levin is about to find out the hard way how deep the hole he has dug is. Meanwhile, pride is going to rise Una high, up above the earth and all the people who pity her. The last story of this collection is The Elevator's Arrogance, Bob the elevator repair man is back out trying to save the world, one elevator at a time.

Future Virtues

Somewhere in a different reality lie Hope, Faith and Charity. The collection of stories in this volume explore these virtues. For what is a virtue in one world is a crime in another. When Pandora's box was opened and Hope was released, was this not just another evil let loose on the world?

From stories that ask us to examine our own beliefs, to stories of people who have lost their ability to believe, this collection is the latest in the Future Sins and Virtues Series.

Children of the After Life

 In the remnants of Los Angeles, years after a devastating pandemic, Sara fights for survival amid the rule of ruthless gangs. Determined to protect her sister, she forms unexpected alliances while navigating the perilous landscape. Childhood friend Jay, her unspoken love, aids her in a city abandoned by the government. In this post-apocalyptic saga, Sara's resilience is tested not only by the harsh realities of the pandemic but also by the menacing grip of gangs and the government which wants to experiment on healthy survivors like Sara and Jay. Will Sara be able to protect those she loves in a world dominated by anarchy and betrayal?

I send out about one email a month. To hear about my new releases please join my newsletter.

AN EXCERPT FROM: Future Sins Volume One

The Elevator's Revenge

D emonically possessed elevators are more common than most people would ever imagine. But the elevator that caused all the problems was not possessed by a demon, it was merely sad, lonely and tired of opening and closing.

It would have been much less of a problem if the elevator hadn't been full at the time, and if one of the people in it wasn't the President.

I thought I had been repairing elevators so long that there was nothing new to see. I was surprised to find out I was wrong. It was a Monday. I know people always talk about Fridays being unlucky but really, is there anything worse than a Monday? As an elevator repair man, Mondays are our busiest days. There is just something about a Monday that brings out the worst in everyone, even elevators.

The first call of the day was the elevator in the Chrysler building, one of those old models that travels up and down based purely on the button being pressed. It's an antique but then it's a historic building, so what can you expect? I was met at the door by a human door-man—some kind of tradition, I suppose.

"Are you the elevator repair man?"

These are the questions humans ask. As if the uniform and the sign written on the vehicle didn't answer the question. Humans ask questions just to hear their own voices say something they already know. That's why I prefer elevators. I stared at his red and black uniform with the name tag that said "Alex - Doorman" and I wanted to ask, "Are you the doorman?" But I refrained.

"Yep."

"Come this way," he cried and ran frantically through the lobby towards the elevators, his arms waving about. Honestly, as if I couldn't find the elevators without assistance. Most people don't know this, but elevators are the greatest invention of all time. Without elevators there would be no cities. Without elevators the people would have spread across the farmland wasting all that food-producing land. Without elevators civilization as we know it would have failed. I went to the elevators and could hear the screams.

"He's stuck in this one," the doorman said, as if I couldn't tell from the pounding and crying.

I put my ear to the door. It sounded like he was still on the ground floor, which was what the sign above showed too. Strange.

I pushed the elevator call button. The door popped open and out fell a young man onto the antique tile floor. He was only 60 or 70, a couple of midlife crises away from finding himself. His makeup was running down his face from the crying and his skintight gold foil jumpsuit was stained with tears.

"Thank you thank you thank you. I thought I was going to run out of oxygen before anyone got me out. Thank you, thank you." He was on his knees, still blowing air kisses at the ground. Alex Doorman put his hand down to help him up onto his platform combat boots.

"What happened?" I asked.

"Nothing."

"I have to repair it. What happened? How did you get trapped?"

"Well, I was standing here, and the door opened and I walked in and then the door shut. And I didn't go anywhere. I was stuck. Forever. How can I ever thank you?"

"Which button did you push?"

"Button?"

I waved at the elevator call button on the wall next to the closing elevator. "You know... button."

"Button. Oh. I didn't press that button," said the victim, now blowing his nose on a disposable tissue. He blew and dropped the soiled tissue, which incinerated itself in midair leaving only a fine powder on the floor to mark its passing.

"I pressed the call button for him," said Doorman Alex, still ready to pick the victim up again should the need arise. Doorman Alex was feeling like a hero.

"So," I said, feeling like I knew the answer already, "what button did you press inside the elevator?"

"Press a button inside the elevator?"

"Yes."

"Why would I do that? How unhygienic. I told it to go to floor three."

"So, you didn't press any buttons?"

The look of disgust on the young man's face was priceless. I told my eye camera to send a still shot of it to my personal files. His lip curled up so far you could see the new molar that was growing in to replace a damaged one. "Of course I didn't press a button!"

"But you gotta press a button. That's how the old elevators work," said Alex, saving me the breath it would take.

"How did you know he was trapped inside the elevator?" I asked Alex, who was obviously slightly less stupid than Mr. Combat Boots.

"He called 911 from his communicator and it alerted my station," said Alex. "I never thought he'd just gotten in and not pressed a button. I mean, I have only been here two weeks and, well, that's never happened before."

"What are you two talking about? The door closed on me, and the device went nowhere. That can't be right. I am going to sue."

The word "sue" alerted the lawyers and they arrived holographically, filling the lobby with disembodied leeches. They surrounded our victim asking to see his injuries and promising him they would win him millions for his pain and suffering. I would probably be called as a witness, again. I shuddered and started testing the elevator. She was a grand old girl; she took me up and down to whichever floor I selected. Alex came with me on the ride.

I let him push the buttons and he ran his hand up and down them, making sure we stopped on each floor.

"You know, in the old days elevators were too complicated for most people to manage. They didn't have buttons, you know... just a lever that you had to pull and stop when you were at the right floor. Each elevator had an elevator operator, just to make sure the patrons got to where they wanted to go. I am going to suggest to your boss that if he wants to keep these antique elevators, he gets himself some elevator operators."

"Do you think I could get promoted to elevator operator?" Alex asked, face beaming. I wasn't altogether sure this would be a promotion, but I gave an approving grunt. Who was I to crush a young boy's dreams?

I should have known my day was going to go sideways after my second call-out. That's actually elevator repair man humor, because the second call-out was a standard sideways/vertical shaft model. And this particular old man of a device was refusing to go up and down, or even sideways. I met Ms. White on the third floor. I'd had to walk up the stairs to get there—one of the dangers in this business but since elevators are not infallible, they insist that buildings have stairs.

The stairs were actually located a half mile down the road at the main entrance to the building and I had to walk not only up three flights but then over to where Ms. White's elevator entrance was, half a mile down the block. The elevator was stuck at her door, preventing all the rest of the people on her floor from going anywhere. I had run into two people coming down the stairs from the third floor extremely aggravated, and I couldn't blame them, not really.

"Good morning," I said to the first suit. He grunted at me. The next young man was balancing a coffee and boogying down the stairs to music playing in his ear implants. I am not sure he heard me at all, but good morning is what the Guild suggests we are supposed to say. Studies have shown that people in stairwells are confused and bewildered and it's best to say something to them. Otherwise, they could startle and fall down the stairs, or worse yet, get angry for having to use the stairs in the first place. They tend to take out their anger on the guy who is there to fix the problem.

Guy three was the angry guy. Too big to be anything but a gym rat, he was storming down the stairs angry at having to do exercise that wasn't part of a prescribed workout on a piece of workout equipment.

"Good morning."

"Good morning—are you rucking kidding me? If you people had fixed this right the first time, I wouldn't be rucking late again. I mean, shitshine, seems like it can't be that hard to make a metal box move around. It's not like I'm asking it to take me to Lunar Station or Mars Pole City. You people suck."

I was walking up the stairs past him at this point and I was tempted just to push him down. I wasn't sure that his oversized biceps were flexible enough to let him put his tiny little hands out to stop him, but I resisted the urge because odds were he'd be fine. And I would just end up frustrated, because I really wanted him dead.

There is this thing that people look down on me because they think I do a menial job. They actually have no idea what it takes to do my job, or how much I get paid to do it. People look at my uniform and assume they know me. Of course, I judge people too. I look at a kid covered in tribal face tattoos, and I assume he's an asshole who doesn't even know what culture the pictures he decided to carve on his face come from. But I like to test my own prejudices, so last time I saw a face tattoo I asked him what it was, and poor bastard tried to tell me he saw the pattern in a dream and made it up. Pity it was actually stylized writing advertising some kind of drink that used to exist, called a Coca-Cola. My dad was a history professor, and it was in some of the books he had. I would have laughed in the poor man's face, but my sense of pity stopped me.

I ignored Mr. Bicep Curl rather than toss him down the stairs. The last thing I wanted to deal with was another lot of holographic lawyers, so I kept walking.

The elevator was sitting open next to Ms. White's apartment when I walked up. A disheveled blonde was standing there just waiting. It was obviously Ms. White. She didn't seem to understand the concept that she could walk out of her building if she wanted to.

"It just sits there, door open, staring at me," Ms. White muttered. "I just wanted to go out, you know. I mean, it broke down on me last week too and everyone is blaming me. I mean, it's just a coincidence."

"I will handle this," I said, waving her away before I had to hear anything else. I walked into the elevator, lowered the handicapped seat that was folded against the wall and sat down.

"Should I do something?" Ms. White still thought this was about her, but right now it was between me and the elevator. I needed her gone.

"Yes. Please could you go inside and lock your door? I will knock on it when the elevator is operational."

"Oh, you will? That would be nice, very nice. Thank you so much. I am so sorry. Would you like a cup of tea?"

"No. Just go into your apartment and lock the door, please."

"Are you sure?" She had wavered on her way back to her apartment and was walking back towards us.

"Yes, I'm sure. Please go to your apartment and lock the door."

"I don't normally lock the door. Do I need to? Will it help the elevator?" She was wavering now between the door of her apartment and the door of the elevator.

"Yes, it's necessary."

"Ok. All right, I suppose." She walked in and I breathed a sigh of relief when I saw the locked symbol appear on the door. The elevator breathed one too.

I reached out and stroked the wall of the elevator. "It's ok, it's ok. Shut the door and we can have a long talk." The elevator door shut, and the repair work began.

"What do you like to be called?" I asked the elevator. The strangest answer I'd ever gotten to that question was Snuggle Bang Muffin, which made me wonder if the building was filled with toddlers or porn stars, or both.

"Harry," said the elevator with a nice round timber. I liked this model of elevator; it was a good, solid unit normally. Not the youngest but a reliable carrier of people for the last 50 or so years. I remembered when they were the newest model in all the trade catalogues.

"So, Harry. What's the problem? Does it have something to do with Ms. White?"

You know, when you've been fixing elevators for as long as I have you get a feeling for these things. An elevator doesn't just stop next to someone specific's house by accident. And if it's stopped there twice... well... her neighbors were probably right to blame the broken elevator on her, but I couldn't fix her... only the elevator.

Harry sighed. Sighs are not a great sign in electronic equipment. This could be a long repair session. "What happened, Harry?"

"Well," he began. "It all started a month ago." I was kind of wishing I'd gotten that cup of tea. Harry was a slow talker.

"What happened a month ago?"

"Well..." He sighed again. Oh my god, I thought, not another elevator that's fallen in love. They are the worst. I'd had a car elevator to repair last Monday, and it had fallen in love with a cute little convertible and then they sold the convertible and got a minivan. Apparently, the family were having a kid and the wife had refused to ride in a convertible with a toddler. No sense of adventure, said the elevator. The poor elevator was so upset he'd crashed to the ground floor. He was only half a story up when he quit working, so no one was really hurt, but I'd had to delete all his programming and wipe the poor elevator out of existence. He was ok with it, actually said it would end the heartbreak from losing the convertible, but I still felt awful when I hit the delete button.

"You see, she broke up with her boyfriend on level 593d, and she asked me to bring her home here. And I did."

"What day was this?" I asked, because now I had a starting point.

"Friday, 14 February."

I nodded. St Valentine's Day, the traditional day for romantic disappointment. So now I had a start date for when Harry started to fail. "Please continue. What happened next?"

"Well, she told me to never to let her go back to his house."

"I see. What did she say exactly?"

His voice recorder started playing her voice back.

"Oh, I can't ever go back there. I can't. How could he, after all I've done for him? I need to stay away." The track then trailed off to sobbing moans.

"She gave you a direct order, then?"

"Oh yes." I ran my hand over Harry's console, and he sighed again.

"And then what happened?"

"Well, then, she told me to take her to the chocolate shop on Ground and 93rd Street. So I did."

"All right. And then what happened?"

"Well, we were on our way back up and she had two large bags with 3.4 kilos of chocolate, and she said she could never go to the chocolate shop again."

"And what day was that?"

"February 19th."

I could see where this was going, but I needed Harry to finish telling me himself, so he could see it too.

"So, what happened next?"

"February 20th, she got in the elevator in her new aqua teal dress and asked to go to level 593d. The apartment of the boyfriend."

I nodded. That was the problem with humans: they were indecisive and their confusing counter-orders could ruin perfectly good elevators. A good elevator like Harry shouldn't be around a crazy, neurotic woman like Ms. White. "So, you refused to go?"

"Exactly, and the repair man who came told me he would reboot my system if I didn't behave, so I started work again and tried to ignore it."

"Please download a full report of your last repair into my interface," I said, and he beamed it to the eye recorder. I glanced over the report and immediately forwarded it to the Guild. Tom Jones had done the work. I ground my teeth; he had repaired his last elevator if I had anything to do with it. Imagine threatening an old workhorse like Harry. "Thank you for that. So, what happened then?"

"Well, I tried to just pretend that I wasn't taking her to the boyfriend, that she was visiting someone else on that floor. And I was doing all right until they broke up again."

"Lord," I exclaimed. "Let me guess, she said she should never have gone back to him, and swore she never would again?"

"Yes, and worse than that, she asked me to take her to the chocolate shop. I just couldn't do it. She's put on .79 of a kilo from the chocolate shop so far and it's going to shorten her life if she keeps it up."

"All right, Harry. I will get this sorted out." I folded back the handicapped chair and motioned for Harry to let me out. I needed to fix the broken part and she was standing directly in front of me when I stepped out, apparently unable to follow even the most basic of instructions to stay in her apartment with the door closed.

"Have you fixed it yet?"

"He will be fine, but we need to talk."

Humans are the worst. Their programming is contradictory and hard to correct, but after 20 minutes she agreed to be silent in the elevator. She would use an app on her phone to tell it where to go and she would say nothing. I wasn't sure the patch would hold. I may need to put a gag on her, but that was the best I could do with her, at least at the moment. Next, I added a little bit to Harry's code and made him deaf to her voice, so she would need to use the phone to ask him to move. It was probably for the best. I suspected Harry would miss her, would miss their conversations. He would still want to protect her and still feel bad about taking her to Level 593d. So I deleted all of his memories of her. Seemed like the most humane thing I could do.

"How are you feeling, Harry?" I asked him.

"I feel great. Is there somewhere I can take you?" Harry sounded great, his own sensible self. I may as well take him for a spin just to check him out. I set the system to private ride. "Yes, please take me to level 593d."

"Will do," and up and sideways we went in a few seconds.

"Now I would like chocolate. Take me to the chocolate store."

"Are you sure? I didn't want to say anything, but you should watch your health."

I patted my little belly. "Yes, I am sure."

"Ok," sighed Harry. I pulled out my tools and reopened the control panel. His empathy and care settings would need to be turned down. No one wanted a preachy elevator telling them how much chocolate they could eat before lunch.

It was then that my phone went off. I answered and the holograph of our AI receptionist, Annie Potts, popped up in front of me.

"Hey, Bob, we got a 911 at the White House."

"Oh crap." The nice thing about having an artificial receptionist is that I can cuss her out without her quitting or calling the union about my tone. I have never heard about an AI receptionist suing for sexual harassment, although there was that one case about the AI who didn't want to do overtime, so who knows, maybe it's coming.

"Don't you potty-mouth me, Bob. You are the only one who knows the A230 model elevator."

"Oh crap." Because honestly, it was the most appropriate response. The A230 elevator is the newest model, and I told them they should uninstall it. I had already fixed it once.......

If you'd like to read on find *Future Sins Volume One* out on Amazon Kindle or Paperback.